The Hardy Boys Mystery Stories

The
Haunted Fort

Franklin W. Dixon

Armada

First published in the U.K. in 1973 by William Collins
Sons & Co. Ltd., London and Glasgow. First published in
Armada 1974 by William Collins Sons & Co. Ltd.,
14 St. James's Place, London, S.W.1.

Printed in Great Britain by
Love & Malcomson Ltd., Brighton Road,
Redhill, Surrey.

CONTENTS

"Look out!" Frank yelled. *"The wall!"*

·1·

Scalp Warning

"CHET MORTON inviting us to a mystery—I don't believe it!" Blond seventeen-year-old Joe Hardy smiled as he and his brother bounded off the back steps towards the garage.

Frank Hardy, dark-haired and a year older than Joe, eagerly keyed the car motor to life. Soon they were headed out of Bayport for the Morton farm. Dusk was falling.

"Chet seemed too excited to say much on the phone," Frank explained. "But he did mention there might be a holiday in it for us—and a haunted fort."

"A haunted fort!"

When the brothers pulled into the gravel driveway of the rambling, brown-and-white farmhouse, pretty Iola Morton, Chet's sister, danced off the porch to greet them.

"Frank and Joe! What a surprise! You're just in time for our folk concert!"

"And I can play two chords!" Callie Shaw waved from the front doorway, a large guitar hanging from her neck. Callie, a slim blonde, was Frank's special friend, while vivacious Iola often dated Joe.

"It sounds great," Frank began, "but Chet called us over to—" He glanced suspiciously at Joe. "Say, do you think these two got Chet to lure us over here about a mystery?"

"Of course not, sillies," dark-haired Iola protested, her eyes snapping. "Besides, who wants to talk about murky old mysteries? Wait until you hear Callie's new ballad records."

As the four entered the house, a round face beneath a coonskin cap peered from the kitchen. Then the stocky figure of Chet Morton made an entrance.

"Hi, Hardys! Anybody for a haunted holiday?"

"Chet! Then there really is a mystery?" Joe's face brightened as Chet nodded and motioned the brothers upstairs to his room. But not before the girls frowned disdainfully.

"Meanies!" Callie said. "Don't be all day!"

As the Hardys took seats, Chet lay back on his bed and began, "My uncle Jim phoned late this afternoon from Crown Lake in New England. You know, he's chief painting instructor at a summer art school there."

Chet explained that the place, named Millwood, was sponsored by a millionaire for the benefit of talented teenagers.

"Sounds like a good arrangement for aspiring artists," Frank remarked.

"Uncle Jim loves his job," Chet continued, "or at least he did before the painting thefts started."

"You mean thefts of students' paintings?" Joe interrupted, puzzled.

"No. Something much more valuable. Uncle Jim didn't go into details, but he did mention somebody called the Prisoner-Painter. Two of his pictures have disappeared."

"What about the local police?" Frank asked.

"They've already tried to solve the case. No luck. That's why Uncle Jim wants us to live at the school for a while."

"How'd he know about us?" Joe put in.

"I mentioned you in my letters. Course, I didn't tell him any of the *bad* things about you—only that you were a couple of great detectives."

Frank grinned and aimed a slow-motion swing towards his teasing pal, but in a flash Chet was on his feet, twirling his coonskin cap. "I'm half-packed already." He brightened, a hopeful look in his eye. "Will you fellows come along?"

"Try and keep us away!" Joe exclaimed. He was as excited as Frank at the prospect of adventure.

Both boys, sons of Bayport's famous detective, Fenton Hardy, had already tackled and solved many mysteries. From the baffling secrets of their first case to their most recent mystery, the boys welcomed each new challenge. Chet, their loyal and close friend, though sometimes reluctant to sleuth with them, often proved to be of great help.

"Chet," Frank added, "didn't you mention a haunted fort on the phone?"

"Oh, that!" Chet groaned. "Yes, I did. Uncle Jim said something about an old French fort nearby, but maybe it's not important. Help, fellows, haunted places don't agree with me!"

"I don't know," Frank mused, winking at Joe. "I hear some ghosts are well fed. Think we could introduce Chet to one or two up at Crown Lake?"

Chet could not repress a smile as the brothers chuckled, then patted him on the back. Suddenly they heard a scream from the front porch.

"That's Callie!" Joe cried out.

The three boys rushed downstairs. Iola stood trembling in the doorway. Callie, pale with fright, pointed to a hairy object on the lawn.

"What happened?" Frank asked in alarm.

Callie said that a speeding black car had slowed in front of the house and somebody had tossed out the object.

"It looks like—like a scalp!" Iola shuddered.

The Hardys rushed out to the lawn and Frank knelt over the strange thing.

"It's a scalp all right—made of papier-mâché! Looks pretty real with all this red paint."

Joe picked it up. "There's a note attached!" He removed a small piece of paper from the underside. Frowning, he read the typewritten words aloud:

" '*Use your heads, stay away from
Crown Lake.*' "

"Did you get a look at the driver?" Frank asked, as Iola and Callie joined the boys.

"No, but I think it was an out-of-state licence plate," Callie replied. "I thought he was just a litter-lout until I saw—*that.*"

The gruesome-looking object was made from black bristles of the sort used in paintbrushes. Frank turned to Chet and Joe. "What do you two make of it?"

Joe shrugged. "Who would want to stop us from going to Crown Lake—and why?"

"Also," Chet added, "how did anybody even know we had been invited up to Crown Lake by my uncle?"

The young people discussed the strange warning as the Hardys returned to their car, where Frank deposited the fake scalp.

"It's a scalp!"

"This grisly clue indicates one thing," Frank concluded. "Somebody wants us to stay away from Millwood Art School! If that's where our 'scalper' is from, it might explain how he learned of Mr Kenyon's invitation."

"Speaking of invitations," Joe said, "what time do you want to leave tomorrow, Chet?"

"Leave!" Iola and Callie exclaimed.

"Sure." Frank grinned. "I've always been interested in Indian haircuts—that is, unless Chet wants to back out."

"Me—back out?" Chet swallowed, then resolutely replaced the coonskin cap on his round head—backwards. "Fur Nose Morton will pick you up tomorrow morning at ten sharp. Don't forget to pack some warm clothes!"

The girls protested in vain. After making the boys promise not to be away for the whole summer, they wished them a safe and pleasant trip. As Frank drove the car down the drive, Joe leaned out the window.

"We'll take you up on that folk concert invitation some time, girls. See you in the morning, Chet!"

Full of anticipation about their new mystery, the Hardys drove directly to their tree-shaded house at the corner of High Street and Elm Street. After securing permission from their parents for the trip to Crown Lake, the excited boys spent the rest of the evening packing three large suitcases. Before going to bed, they quickly read several school-books on the history of the Crown Lake region. It had been an area of conflict during the French and Indian War.

"Here's a fort!" Joe remarked. "Senandaga! That may be the place Chet's uncle mentioned. According to this, Senandaga was an impressive stronghold, though it didn't play a large role in the campaigns."

"If a fort's haunted, we can't expect it to be historical too," Frank grinned.

"Wait a minute!" Joe looked up. "There's a small painting of this fort right in the Bayport Museum!"

"The same one?"

"Yes. What say we have a look at it tomorrow before Chet gets here?"

After a sound night's sleep the boys awoke half an hour earlier than usual the following morning and quickly arranged their luggage on the front porch. Leaving word that they would be back by ten, they drove down to the Bayport Museum.

A small, pug-faced man carrying a large sketch pad was just leaving the building as they reached the top of the marble steps. After bumping into Frank, he bowed nervously, then hastened down the steps and up the street.

"He's sure an early-bird artist," Joe remarked.

They passed into the cool, echoing foyer and were just about to enter the American Collection Room when they heard running footsteps and a cry for help. A distraught, bespectacled man waved to them and pointed ahead.

"That man—stop him—he's stolen our fort painting!"

· 2 ·

Highway Chase

"FORT painting!" The words set Frank and Joe racing after the thief. They darted outside and down the marble steps three at a time! Frank went in one direction, Joe the other. But there was no sign of the fugitive.

After the Hardys had checked several side streets, they headed back and met at the museum.

"No luck," Frank said.

"He must have had a car," Joe declared.

"Another thing," Frank said, "I'll bet he hid the painting in that big sketch pad of his."

In the foyer of the museum, the brothers were questioned by two policemen. After Frank and Joe had given their statements to the officers, they spoke with the museum director, the man who had alerted them to the theft. As Frank suspected, the thief had apparently concealed the small painting in his sketch pad.

"I don't know why he chose the picture of Fort Senandaga," the director lamented, "but I'm sorry he did. So far as I know, ours was the only work of the Prisoner-Painter in this area."

The Hardys started in surprise. This was the same artist whose pictures had been disappearing from Millwood Art School!

After the director had thanked them for their efforts, they returned to their car, each with the same thought: Had the morning's theft any connection with the art school mystery?

When they reached home, Chet was sitting disconsolately on the porch steps fanning himself with a blue beret.

"Leaping lizards! What a morning you fellows pick for going to a museum," he moaned. "I could have had a second breakfast while I've been waiting for you."

"We're sorry, Chet," Frank apologized, "but it turned out to be a longer stint than we'd reckoned."

While the Hardys loaded their bags into Chet's freshly polished yellow jalopy, the Queen, they told him of the museum theft. Chet whistled.

"Do you think the thief's the one who threw that scalp on our lawn?"

"It's likely," Frank replied.

When the jalopy had been loaded up to the back window, Mrs Hardy came out and embraced the boys warmly. "Do take care of yourselves." She smiled. "Dad will be home in a few days. I'll tell him about your case, but I feel sure you can solve it by yourselves."

Amid goodbyes, Chet backed the car down the drive, and soon the jalopy was headed north out of Bayport. After following the county road for half an hour, Chet guided the car on to the wide-laned state motorway extending like a white ribbon beneath a light-blue sky.

The boys conversed excitedly about their destination and the mystery to be solved there.

"You really have done a tune-up job on the Queen,

Chet," Joe commented from the back seat. "One of these days she may threaten to approach the speed limit."

Chet smiled good-naturedly at the gibe, then frowned, tugging at his beret to keep it from being blown off by the brisk wind. Finally he gave up. "Alas, what we artists must bear." He sighed and stuffed the cap into the glove compartment.

Frank grinned. "What happened to that coonskin job you had yesterday?"

"Oh," Chet said airily, "I thought I'd get into the artistic spirit."

As they drove by a roadside café and service station a black saloon pulled out from the access lane into the one for slow-moving traffic. As Chet moved over to the middle lane to pass, Joe glanced at the saloon and sat up sharply.

"Frank! The driver of that car—it's the picture thief!"

Immediately Chet slackened speed. Looking over, Frank too recognized the pug-faced man at the wheel an instant before the thief saw the Hardys. Clearly alarmed, the man pressed the accelerator and the black car shot ahead, but Frank glimpsed in its back seat a large sketch pad!

"Stay with him!" Joe urged, as the gap widened between the two cars. Futilely, Chet pushed the Queen's old pedal to the floor, then he noticed a large sign to the right: PAY TOLL—½ MILE.

"Quick, a quarter!"

Ahead, they could see the black car slow down at the exact-change booth to the right. Chet closed the space quickly before the other car moved ahead, less swiftly this time. Beyond the toll, a parked State Police car was visible.

"Now's our chance to catch him!" Frank exclaimed. Chet pulled up to the same booth and hastily flipped the coin into the collection basket. Without waiting the second for the light to turn green, he drove the Queen in hot pursuit of the black car.

Ahead, a blast of exhaust smoke told the pursuers that the thief was piling on the speed. As Chet strained over the wheel trying to narrow the gap he heard a siren behind him, and the trooper waved the jalopy to the roadside.

"What happened?" Joe asked anxiously as Chet stopped.

The trooper pulled ahead, got out, and ambled over. "It's customary to drop a quarter in the toll basket, young fellow."

"I did."

The trooper looked annoyed. "The light is still red, and besides, the alarm bell rang."

"But—but—" Chet spluttered in surprise.

"Let's see your licence."

"Officer," Frank spoke up, "we're in a hurry. We're chasing a thief!"

The trooper smiled in spite of himself. "Well, I've never heard that one before."

"But we are!" Joe insisted. "A painting was stolen in Bayport."

"You can check with Chief Collig there," said Frank.

The trooper eyed the trio suspiciously. "Okay. But if this is a hoax, I'll arrest all three of you." He strode to his car and spoke into the radio. Three minutes later he trotted back. "Accept my apologies, boys. You were right. Can you describe that car?"

As Joe gave the information, including the licence number which he had memorized, Chet hurried to the toll basket. He returned waving a cloth in his hand. "That's a clever crook!" he shouted. "He dropped this rag in the basket so my quarter wouldn't register."

"He won't get away from us," the trooper said. He ran to his car, radioed to police ahead, then sped off at ninety miles an hour.

"Now we've got action," Frank said as Chet urged the Queen along the motorway.

Twenty minutes later as they left the motorway, they saw the trooper parked alongside the road. Chet pulled up behind him.

"Sorry, boys!" the officer called out. "The thief gave us the shake. But we'll track him down!"

After a brief stop at a snack bar the trio continued on towards Crown Lake, with Frank at the wheel.

The flat countryside gave way to ranges of dark and light green hills, several of them arching spectacularly up on either side of the broad road, curving towards the blue sky.

An hour later they left the main road and proceeded through several small towns before sighting the bluish-grey water of Crown Lake. It first appeared partially screened by a ridge of trees, then came into full view at a rise, just beyond which there was a dirt road and a sign: MILLWOOD ART SCHOOL 500 YARDS AHEAD TO THE RIGHT. Frank swung into the road and in a few minutes the sloping green lawns of the estate came into view. Frank pulled into a parking area facing the edge of the slope and stopped beside a large oak.

Chet led the way vigorously down a gravelled path which wound across the grounds. "Uncle Jim's teaching his class now," he called back to the Hardys.

Ahead, on a level stretch of lawn, the trio saw a group of young people standing in front of easels. Near one student stood a tall, husky, blond-haired man in a painting smock. When he saw the boys, he beamed and hurried over.

"Chet! Good to see you again!"

"Hello, Uncle Jim!" Chet promptly introduced Frank and Joe to Mr Kenyon, who shook hands warmly.

"Welcome to Millwood," he smiled. "Fortunately, my last class today is finishing, and I can help you with your luggage."

The painting instructor accompanied the boys back across the lawn towards the uphill path. Suddenly one of the students cried out:

"Look out! That car—it's rolling!"

A shudder passed through the boys as they saw the yellow Queen rolling down the slope from the parking area. Directly in its path two girls stood rooted in terror at their easels.

Chet's jalopy gathered speed. It hurtled faster and faster towards the girls!

"We've got to stop it!" shouted Joe, on the run.

·3·

Inquisitive Student

JOE sprinted across the slope and dived for the car. Hanging on, he reached through the window and wrenched at the wheel. The Queen swerved, missed the girls by inches, crushed the easels, and came to rest in a tangle of thick underbrush.

Then Joe ran up to the frightened students. "Are you all right?" he asked with concern.

Both girls nodded, trembling with relief. One said, "We owe you our lives!"

"And our paintings too," said her companion.

Their two half-finished canvases had been knocked off the easels and lay intact, face up on the ground.

By now Frank, Chet, and Mr Kenyon had rushed over. "Are you all right, Joe?"

"I'm fine, but I'd rather tackle a whole football team than a runaway car!"

The praises of the onlookers for his bravery embarrassed Joe. "Let's find out what happened to the Queen," he said.

The boys found the car undamaged. "Hey!" Chet cried out. "The emergency's off! I know you set it, Frank."

The jalopy was driven back to the parking area.

This time it was left well away from the rim of the incline. Frank looked around.

"The car didn't just happen to roll. Somebody deliberately released the emergency brake."

Mr Kenyon frowned. "What a terrible prank!"

"I don't believe it was a practical joke," Frank said. "What the motive was, though, I can't guess yet."

The boys took their luggage from the car, and then Mr Kenyon led them towards a small, newly painted building. "I'm sorry you had to be welcomed to Millbrook in this manner," he said. "But we'll try to make up for it."

He took the visitors through a side door into a large, cluttered room, piled with dusty easels, rolls of canvas, and cardboard boxes filled with paint tubes. "This is our storage house," explained the art instructor.

The boys followed him down a narrow stairway into a small basement studio. The stone room smelled of oil paints. Several unframed modern paintings lay along one wall. Mr Kenyon reached up with a pole to open the single window near the ceiling.

"This is my little garret—subterranean style," he explained. "Make yourselves comfortable. Since the thefts, I've been living upstairs where I have a better view of our art gallery across the way."

The boys set down their bags on three sturdy bunks. Joe grinned. "I'm beginning to feel like an artist."

"So am I," Frank said. "This room is fine, Mr Kenyon."

"Just call me Uncle Jim. How about supper? You must be hungry."

Chet beamed. "I could eat an easel!"

First, however, he eagerly recounted the scalp incident to his uncle, then the Hardys told of their experiences at the Bayport Museum and on the motorway. Mr Kenyon agreed there probably was a connection with the Millwood thefts.

"But the man you describe doesn't ring any bells with me," he continued. "Our summer session had been going along well until five days ago when I discovered a painting was missing from our small gallery. The day before yesterday, a second was stolen during the night—both works of the Prisoner-Painter." He sighed. "We have to keep the building under lock and key now, even from our students."

"So tomorrow we'll start our sleuthing," said Joe.

"Right. Perhaps by mingling with the students you can pick up some clue," replied Uncle Jim. "Though I'd hate to suspect any of them."

"Can you tell us about this Prisoner-Painter?" Frank asked.

"I could," Mr Kenyon said, smiling, "but I think Mr Jefferson Davenport would rather tell you himself, since the artist is his ancestor."

"The wealthy man who started Millwood?" Joe put in.

"Yes. He looks forward to meeting you detectives, but he won't be receiving visitors today, because of the anniversary of a battle."

"A battle?" Frank echoed in surprise.

The instructor chuckled. "You'll find Mr Davenport is quite an authority on the science of military fortification, in addition to his interest in painting. You'll see when you meet him tomorrow."

"What about this haunted fort?" Joe asked eagerly.

"Senandaga?" Uncle Jim's eyes twinkled. "There are apparently some weird on-goings there. But Mr Davenport will fill you in on that, too."

Uncle Jim then took the Hardys and Chet to the Davenport lakeside mansion, an old gabled house staffed only by a woman cook and a part-time chauffeur-gardener.

"Mr Davenport has invited us to have meals in the kitchen during your stay here," the instructor said.

After a hearty supper Mr Kenyon took the boys on a tour. He explained that the Millwood grounds were tended by the students themselves, who rented rooms in the nearby village of Cedartown. Art materials, all instruction, and part of rent costs were financed by the millionaire patron. Several townspeople also painted on weekends at the school.

Uncle Jim showed his visitors the studios, the gallery building from the outside, and finally, a boathouse near the mansion. Several canoes were tied up to a jetty. These, Mr Kenyon said, were for the students' use.

As he accompanied the boys back to their quarters the instructor said with a grin, "Don't expect Mr Davenport to be too—er—ordinary." He did not explain further, and bade them good night, saying the art patron expected them to call at nine a.m. the next day.

Early the next morning Joe awoke to see an unfamiliar face peering down into their room through the single, high window. The boy, who appeared to be about nineteen, scowled at Joe, then disappeared.

At that moment Frank awakened.

"What's the matter?" he asked his brother, who was sitting up in bed staring at the window.

"Some fellow was looking in here. He didn't seem the cheerful type."

Frank laughed. "One of the students, probably. Maybe he's envious of our artist's garret. Let's wake up Chet and get some vittles."

After breakfast the three boys strolled round the grounds, already dotted with students setting up easels or heading for studio classes. Joe stared as he noticed one student, carrying a small easel, approaching them.

"He's the one I saw at the window this morning!"

Like many of the other students, the boy wore a grey smock. His face, long and with pudgy lips, had a faintly insolent expression. He came up to the boys.

"You new here?" he asked, his eyes narrowing.

"Yes," Frank answered. "We plan to pick up some painting tips as guests of Mr Kenyon." He introduced himself and the others.

The student stared at them speculatively. "Oh, is that so? Well, my name's Ronnie Rush." He went on sullenly, "Kenyon would have to lock up the whole gallery just because two measly paintings are gone. I could be doing some research." He shrugged and said off-handedly, "Guess I got nothing against you fellows, though. See you around."

Before the Hardys or Chet could retort, the student shuffled off.

"He's got some nerve," Chet said indignantly, "criticizing Uncle Jim! And why was he looking in our window, anyway?"

"I don't know," Frank said, "but he certainly seems curious about us."

At that moment Uncle Jim, wearing a fresh white

smock, came over and greeted the boys cheerfully. He immediately led them in the direction of the Davenport mansion.

"I'm heading for my watercolour class," he explained, "but you sleuths can have a private conference about our mystery with Mr Davenport."

The instructor led them on to the porch, through the open front door, and pointed down the wood-panelled hall to a large double door at the end.

"That's Mr Davenport's study, where he's expecting you. We'll get together later!"

After Chet's uncle had left, they walked quietly down the hall to the study. Frank knocked. A few seconds later a voice from within said, "Come in."

The boys entered, closed the doors, and found themselves in a high-ceilinged room with heavily draped windows. Bookshelves lined one wall behind a cluttered mahogany desk. The adjacent wall contained a blackboard.

As their eyes became accustomed to the gloom, Joe gave Frank a nudge. "Look there!" he whispered.

Standing on a hassock was a small, grey-haired man in a white summer suit. He held a long pointer in one hand and was looking down at a fort structure of toy logs set up on the floor.

"Never! Never!" exclaimed the man as he collapsed the fort with a swish of the stick.

The trio watched, mouths agape. The man looked up quickly and said, "Hello, boys."

"Mr Davenport?" Chet said, nonplussed.

"I am. And you are James Kenyon's nephew Chester, I believe, and the two Hardy boys! Much honoured!" The man jumped down and shook each boy's hand, bowing slightly. He spoke in a pleasant Southern drawl, but his twinkling blue eyes revealed a lively personality.

"Have a seat," Mr Davenport said.

"We appreciate your invitation to Millwood," Frank said as they settled in comfortable chairs.

"Poor strategy," the art patron muttered. He threw open the draperies and paced the room.

"Pardon, sir?" Joe hesitated.

"Vicksburg, of course," Mr Davenport answered, frowning at the scattered toy logs. "Yesterday was my annual Vicksburg Day."

"Have you many military—er—holidays in the year, Mr Davenport?" asked Chet.

"Fifty-seven, not a one more!" he replied. "Used to have fifty-six till I admitted Bunker Hill this year. Sad days, many of 'em, but—"

Mr Davenport paused. Suddenly he rushed over to the toy logs, reshuffled them into a fort, then stretched out on the floor, sighting along his pointer. Chet watched in bewilderment while the Hardys exchanged smiles. Indeed, Mr Davenport was not ordinary!

Seconds later, the millionaire leaped up. "Terrible defence. It would never hold! Never!" Crouching, he squinted at the logs with his face almost to the floor. Holding the pointer like a cue, he again toppled the logs.

Seating himself in a rocker, the art patron sighed heavily, hooked his thumbs in his waistcoat pockets, and peered earnestly at his callers. "Now, what were you saying?"

Frank hastily told him about the scalp warning and the escaped museum thief. Upon hearing of the stolen Senandaga painting, the elderly man became upset and again paced the room.

"Could you tell us something about the Prisoner-Painter, Mr Davenport?" Joe asked. "And the fort, too?" At that instant Frank heard a faint sound and saw the double door of the study open a fraction of an inch!

"An eavesdropper!" he thought. Frank rushed across the room, but already footsteps were racing down the hall. Grabbing the knobs, he flung the doors wide open.

·4·

A Crimson Clue

STUMBLING footsteps sounded at the bottom of the high
porch, but by the time Frank dashed outside, the
eavesdropper had vanished.

Disappointed, he returned to the others in the study.
"Whoever he was, he didn't drop any clues," Frank
reported.

"You're alert, boys," Mr Davenport commented.
"I like that. What's more, you're not afraid, like that
custodian who guarded my fort."

"*Your* fort?" Joe asked in surprise.

"Yes, young man, Senandaga belongs to me."

"What happened to the custodian?" asked Frank.

"He left. Quit. Said he couldn't stand all that
haunting—queer noises and so forth. To hear him
talk, there's a whole regiment of ghosts manning
the parapets." Mr Davenport looked thoughtful. "Of
course, he claims he had some close calls."

"Such as?" Frank queried.

"Said chunks of masonry nearly fell on him a
couple of times. But"—the art patron looked sceptical—
"I don't put much stock in that."

"Now nobody takes care of the fort?" Joe asked.

"Nobody. And there aren't any nuisances of visitors,
either," Davenport said with satisfaction. "Anyhow,

31

we have enough to do tracking down the art thieves without worrying about the fort."

Then the boys asked Mr Davenport about his ancestor, the Prisoner-Painter.

"Jason Davenport was a great soldier," he began. "When hostilities broke out between the North and the South, he rose quickly to brigadier general. Then, in one rally near the Potomac, he broke the Union line but penetrated too far without logistical support and was captured. He was held prisoner for the duration at the fort."

"A brave man," Joe said. "An ancestor to be proud of."

"The fort is south of here on Crown Lake, isn't it?" Frank asked.

Mr Davenport nodded, motioning towards the large window. "If it weren't for the promontory nearby, you could see Senandaga." He reflected. "Jason Davenport died shortly after the war ended. But had he not been a prisoner there, there wouldn't be the seventeen canvases of Fort Senandaga, three of which," he added in a rueful tone, "have been stolen."

Mr Davenport explained that the general had taken up painting to while away the days. He was a popular hero, well liked by his captors, and received many special favours, including the art materials necessary for his new interest.

"He showed a real genius in imagining different views of the fort from the surrounding countryside."

"And that's why his paintings are valuable enough to tempt a thief?" Joe asked, impressed.

"I'd like to think so," Mr Davenport answered, "but I fear that's not the real reason. You see, there were rumours later that Jason had discovered an old French treasure in the fort—and that he had left a clue to its hiding place. My father and uncle didn't believe it, but *I* did. So I bought the fort two years ago from a private party."

"The general left this clue in a painting?" Chet guessed.

"Yes. Either in the picture itself, or the frame." The art patron went on to explain that his forebear had fashioned a very unusual frame, which he used for all his paintings. "The frames themselves are valuable," he said. "Unfortunately, some of the originals have been lost over the years, so a few of the fort pictures in our gallery are conventionally framed."

Joe asked how many of the general's works were in the school's possession.

"Fourteen."

"Who has the others?"

Mr Davenport's face turned an angry red. "One, I'm sorry to say, belongs to a person who doesn't deserve it." Suddenly, however, he chortled. "But I'll get back at him."

The boys were mystified, but before they could question him, the elderly man added, "Another fort picture belongs to a hermit fellow, an Englishman. He bought the painting years ago at an auction. Lives out on Turtle Island."

"And nobody has found a trace of any clue so far?" Frank asked.

"Not a one. I've been trying to find the fort treasure ever since I came here."

"What is it?" Frank asked. "Jewels?"

"Oh, no. A boom chain, such as those used with

logs for blocking ships in the French and Indian War, when Senandaga was built." The man picked up two of the toy logs and seemed lost in thought for a moment. "Marvellous, marvellous idea, those log-and-chain defences!"

"Could even a historical chain be tremendously valuable?" Joe enquired, to lead Mr Davenport back to the main subject of discussion.

"This one is!" the man returned emphatically. "It's called *chaîne d'or*—a chain of solid gold."

"Gold!" The three sleuths chorused.

Their host explained that in 1762 the proud Marquis Louis de Chambord, builder and commander of Senandaga, had ordered the chain to be forged, not to be used of course, but as a symbol of his fort's strength. There was a disagreement, however, among historians over whether the *chaîne d'or* actually had been made.

"I'm of the firm opinion that it was," he concluded, "which is why I had James invite you boys up here— to track down the art thief and uncover the gold treasure. So, boys, feel free to come and go as you please in my home."

"Could one of Millwood's students be the thief?" Frank asked hesitantly.

The art patron shook his head sadly. "Can't believe it. They're all fine young people! Which reminds me— young people get hungry. How about lunch?"

On a lakeside terrace the three detectives were served club sandwiches and iced tea. As they ate, Frank questioned their host about his cook and chauffeur.

"I trust them implicitly. Both came with excellent references."

The meal over, Frank, Joe, and Chet thanked Mr Davenport and walked back to the school. There, Frank pointed to a long building nestling in a grove of birches.

"What say we look for clues right where the paintings disappeared—the gallery?"

"Good idea," Joe agreed. They crossed a wide lawn and eagerly headed for the old stone structure. Reaching it, Frank used the key given him by Mr Kenyon and opened the large padlock. The boys filed inside and closed the door.

The interior was dim and cool, but sunlight came through the panes of a skylight to brighten the three windowless walls, on which were hung some fifty paintings. The wall at the far end of the room contained General Davenport's, each of which showed a different view of Fort Senandaga.

The boys now noticed the distinctive frames mentioned by the art patron. Their corners jutted out in a diamond shape.

"Look!" Joe pointed to a large yellowed diagram, half of which was torn off. It hung near the fort pictures. "That must be Senandaga."

The Hardys and Chet went over to examine the ancient parchment. Beneath was a label explaining the remnant was from one of the original drawing plans for the fort. Despite the missing part, they could see enough to tell that its layout resembled the form of a star.

"The Prisoner-Painter made his frames roughly in the same shape," Joe observed.

Frank nodded, then said, "I'm sure the police searched here, but anyway, let's take a look around ourselves for a clue to the thief."

Chet took the end wall, Frank and Joe the sides. On their knees, the boys combed the stone floor, then studied the walls for possible telltale marks.

After an hour, their efforts had proved fruitless. "There's still the wall round the entrance," Joe said with a sigh. "Let's inspect every stone."

While Frank examined an empty desk, Chet and Joe pored carefully over the wall. No luck there.

"Say, fellows," Joe suddenly exclaimed, "what about the fort paintings themselves? If the thief was undecided about which one to take, he may have touched some."

"You're right!" Frank agreed. They rushed across to the row of aged canvases. Removing the paintings from the wall, they began inspecting the backs and edges of the frames.

"Look! I've found something!" Chet called out.

Across the paper backing was a sticky smear of red oil paint! "This was made recently," Joe observed. "It still has a strong paint odour."

"There's no fingerprint on the smear," remarked Frank, looking at it closely, before rubbing some of the paint on to a small piece of paper.

"I wonder if the thief is an artist himself," Chet said.

The three left the gallery, and locked the door behind them. The next step, they agreed, would be to identify the paint, then track down the person who used it.

"Except for Uncle Jim and Mr Davenport," Frank cautioned, "we'll keep this clue to ourselves."

Millwood students were now strolling from their classes, and Ronnie Rush emerged from a knot of chatting young artists.

"Pick up many painting tips today?" he asked, setting down his easel. "I see you rated getting into the gallery."

"We've just been on a tour," Frank answered, deftly concealing the paint sample in the palm of his hand. "How about you?"

"Oh, I've been working on a couple of oils," Ronnie said importantly. "Want to see 'em?"

"Not right now," Joe replied. "We're busy. Thanks anyway."

Ronnie looked annoyed and eyed the three boys sullenly as they hurried to their quarters. There they found Jim Kenyon in the storage room shifting art equipment about. He was keenly interested in the paint sample, and congratulated them on finding the clue. He immediately identified the paint.

"It's called alizarin crimson," he said. "Many of our students use it."

"Pretty hard to pinpoint the culprit," Frank observed. "But we won't give up."

After washing his hands in turpentine and soap, the husky instructor accompanied the boys to supper. A tasty meal awaited them in the Davenport kitchen.

After supper the boys went to the lakeside for a look at the boathouse. They peered up at the promontory behind which Fort Senandaga lay.

"Let's go over to the fort tomorrow," Frank suggested. "Right now, we might do some boning up on art. It might sharpen our eyes to finding that treasure clue."

In their basement room, Chet and the Hardys spent the evening mulling over books on painting borrowed from Mr Kenyon. Later, they went upstairs for a conference with Chet's uncle. Using paints and a canvas, the instructor illustrated various art techniques.

"Want to try your hand, Chet?" Mr Kenyon offered, holding out the brush to his nephew. He winked at Frank and Joe. "I think he has the makings of a painter, don't you?"

But before either Hardy could answer, the building shook with a deafening roar that reverberated up the stairwell!

Frank jumped to his feet. "That came from downstairs!" The smell of burnt powder reached them as they all charged down the narrow steps. When they entered their room, Chet gasped.

The wall near which their luggage lay was splattered with red dots!

"A shotgun!" Joe exclaimed, picking up a used cartridge under the window. He grimaced and held out the shell. "Look." Everyone gasped. It was covered with red.

"B-blood?" Chet quavered.

His uncle examined the cartridge. "No. Red paint—alizarin crimson!"

On the floor lay a small paintbrush. Wrapped round it was a piece of paper. Frank unfolded the sheet to disclose a typewritten message:

A mural for the Hardy Boys. Leave Millwood or my next painting will be a coffin—yours.

· 5 ·

Danger Alley

CHET looked nervous. "Another threat!" he exclaimed. "I guess that scalp warning wasn't any joke."

Uncle Jim's face showed concern. "Whoever stuck a gun barrel through that window wants to scare you boys off—that's plain."

Joe said wryly, "Lucky we weren't on hand for the barrage."

Frank compared the note with that found earlier on the scalp. "Both were done on the same typewriter—and this red paint looks like that 'blood' on the papier-mâché."

With flashlights the instructor and the three boys searched the ground outside the shattered window, but no clues were found.

While the boys swept up the broken glass and fallen plaster, they speculated on the identity of their mysterious enemy. The Hardys felt he might very well be the same person who had thrown the scalp and stolen the fort painting in Bayport.

Chet gulped. "You mean—that man trailed us here?" Then he asked, "Do you think snoopy Ronnie Rush could have had something to do with this?" He told his uncle of their encounters with the boy.

"Well," said Mr Kenyon, "Ronnie's sometimes a

39

little hard to work with, but I don't think he'd do something like this. Our annual outdoor exhibition is to be held on Senandaga Day—next Saturday. I'll be pretty busy getting ready for it, so I won't have much time to help you detectives."

Uncle Jim explained that Senandaga Day was celebrated every year. The town decreed that the fort be opened at this time to the public. "By having our art exhibition then, we attract more visitors."

The Hardys decided to track down if possible the source of the empty cartridge. Frank obtained from Uncle Jim the name of a Cedartown hunting equipment shop, the only one in the area.

"It's run by Myles Warren," the painter added. "He's one of our weekend painters, by the way."

Before retiring, the Hardys fastened some slats across the window. The rest of the night passed uneventfully. After breakfast the next morning, the three attended the quaint little church in town and located the shop of Myles Warren.

"We'll come here first thing tomorrow," Frank said.

Back at the school, the boys had midday dinner, then strolled across the lawn towards several students at work on their paintings.

Frank said in a low tone, "Let's see who has been using the alizarin red." The trio split up. Each boy had a paper bearing a smear of the paint. They began browsing near easels set up not only on the main lawn, but also in various nooks on the outskirts of the estate.

"Wow!" Chet exclaimed to himself, coming upon a dazzling creation being worked on by a thin, red-haired boy in dungarees. The plump boy tried to make some order out of the reddish-brown swirls and zig-zag silver streaks. "Looks like a vegetable cart that's been hit by lightning."

The student paused and greeted Chet. "Like it?" He smiled. "It's a meadow in wintertime."

"Oh—er—very unusual." Chet walked on, muttering, "Guess I'll have to get the hang of this stuff."

He stopped at several other easels, some of which bore landscape scenes, and others, views of the Mill-wood buildings or of the surrounding lakes.

"Hi!" A round-faced jovial girl peeked out at Chet from behind an easel. "Are you a new student at Millwood?" she asked, wiping some red paint from her hands on to a rag. Chet explained that he was trying to pick up some pointers.

"You'll have to see our exhibition," she said brightly. "I'm just touching up my portrait. One of the other students modelled for it."

"Is that alizarin crimson?"

"Oh, you! You're an old pro to recognize it," the girl said.

Chet gulped. "She's so nice, she couldn't be the thief," he thought, then peered wide-eyed at the bizarre maze of green and yellow triangles, wavy black lines, blobs of thick red shading, and one eye.

"You say another student modelled for you? Is he all right now?"

The girl giggled. "Quit teasing. You know well enough this is an *abstract*!"

"Oh, yes, of course." Chet smiled and moved on to inspect several other students' canvases before meeting the Hardys near the gallery. "Hope you fellows had more luck than I did," he said.

Frank shook his head. "Everybody is using alizarin crimson. We can't narrow down this clue."

The next morning they walked up the shady lake road to the quaint village of Cedartown. Picturesque shops, the small church, and a barn-like playhouse graced the narrow main street. Frank pointed out the Cedar Sports Store on the other side.

"If the shotgun shell was bought anywhere in the area, there's a good chance it was here," he said. They crossed and entered the dimly lighted shop.

A long, cluttered counter extended along a dusty wall hung with assorted hunting and fishing equipment. Frank rang the counter bell, and a slender hawk-nosed man with a full black beard emerged from a back room.

"Mr Warren?" Frank enquired.

"Yes. What can I do for you?" he asked, smiling. He spread his hands on the counter and looked with interest at the boys.

"Can you tell us whether this was sold here?" Joe asked, handing him the paint-marked cartridge.

The owner pulled a pair of glasses out of his shirt pocket, put them on, and looked closely at the shell. He shook his head and handed it back.

"If it was used in this area, it's probably my stock," Warren affirmed. "But I sell hundreds of this brand to hunters. Although without the red paint," he added, chuckling.

"Then you have no way of pinpointing the customer?" Frank asked.

"I'm afraid not." The man then asked, "You all up here for the fishing? It's great at the north end of the lake."

Frank shook his head. "Just visiting."

After thanking the dealer, the three left the shop. The next moment they heard a cry of anguish from an antique shop across the street. Its owner stood in the doorway waving his arms frantically. "Help! Thief! Help!"

"Over there!" Joe yelled.

Directly opposite, a small man was running into a cobblestone alley. He carried a picture frame under his arm. The boys sprinted across the street and up the lane. They were closing the gap when the man stopped at a parked black sedan. The Hardys gasped.

It was the man who had stolen the fort painting from the Bayport Museum!

"He's got an old fort frame!" Frank cried out, recognizing the odd shape.

The boys put on more speed as the thief hopped into the car and started the motor.

The sedan roared down the lane directly towards the boys! "Quick, this way!" Joe yelled.

They darted to the right and flattened themselves against a building. The speeding vehicle almost brushed them. In a moment it had screeched round the corner and disappeared up the main street.

A curious crowd had gathered, but were quickly dispersed by a policeman. The Hardys and Chet then went with the officer to the antique shop. The owner explained that the pug-faced man, whom he had never seen before, had offered to purchase the frame. Upon hearing the price, the man had said that it was too high, and started towards the door.

"So I went back into my workshop," the dealer continued, "and returned just in time to see that scoundrel making off with the frame." He groaned. "An irreplaceable loss."

Next, the boys were taken to police headquarters, where they told their story to the chief. He said a state alarm would be issued for the fugitive. Since the earlier alert, sent out right after the boys' chase on the motorway, the police had discovered through the licence number that the sedan was stolen.

"We know the fellow's in this area now," the chief said. "We'll keep you boys informed."

Walking back to Millwood, the three discussed the stolen frame.

"Probably," Frank remarked, "the thief didn't have any luck finding a treasure clue in the paintings."

Joe looked thoughtful, "You think this guy stole the gallery pictures, too?"

Frank stared at his brother. "Say! He could be in league with someone else!"

Back at Millwood, Chet and the Hardys told Mr Kenyon of the Cedartown incident. "Pretty bold move," he commented, "risking a theft in broad daylight."

"Well," Joe said glumly, "let's hope the treasure clue isn't in *that* frame."

After some further discussion of the new development in the mystery, Uncle Jim said, "How would you like to get your first look at Fort Senandaga?"

"You bet!"

"Good. Mr Davenport has asked us to go."

The boys and the instructor went to the mansion, where they were introduced to Alex, the millionaire's chauffeur-gardener. Dressed in blue uniform and cap, and tall, with a clipped black moustache, he bowed stiffly to the boys, then moved round to the rear door of a polished limousine.

"Boy, we're going to ride in real style!" Chet exclaimed. "Old Queen will be jealous."

Mr Davenport came out, greeted them cordially, and they all took seats in the back. Soon the limousine was heading south along the pretty, winding lake road. Past the end of the lake, the car turned up a gentle hill and paused at a PRIVATE PROPERTY sign. Alex got out and unlocked a wire gate. The entire south end of the fort promontory was enclosed by fencing marked with NO TRESPASSING signs.

As they drove ahead through overgrown woods, the elderly Southerner spoke proudly of Fort Senandaga's history. He explained that little was known of the one battle fought there between the British and French.

"There's dispute to this day about its outcome," he went on, "and which side was the last to leave the fort. That's probably why some folks believe Senandaga is haunted—ghosts of soldiers from both forces still fighting, no doubt." He added, "Someday I aim to have that fort fully restored."

Chet asked if the public often visited the site at other times besides Senandaga Day. Davenport's face turned livid and his eyes blazed. "The—the public!" he spluttered, sitting up and thumping his cane on the floor. Chet sat petrified until his uncle put a warning finger to his lips and smoothly changed the subject.

Alex parked in a small clearing and everyone got out. The chauffeur stayed with the car. Mr Davenport, his composure restored, led the others to a grass bluff. "There she is!"

The entire lake could be seen, dotted in the distance with islands like scrubby green battleships. To the boys' left, up a gentle slope, rose the stone fort, an expansive star-shaped ruin surrounded by a shallow ditch, overgrown with brush. Although much of the masonry was crumbling, all the walls were at least partially intact.

As they walked towards the ramparts, Chet's uncle pulled the boys aside and accounted for his employer's sudden outburst.

"I guess I should have warned you," he said, chuckling. "There are two things you should never mention in Mr Davenport's presence. One is admitting the public to his fort—he has a great fear that someone will get careless wandering around the ruins and be injured. The other is Chauncey Gilman."

"Chauncey Gilman? Who is he?" Joe asked.

Before Uncle Jim could answer, Mr Davenport summoned them all down the steep counterscarp, or exterior slope of the ditch. As they proceeded, the elderly man talked excitedly.

"Good walls, these," he pointed out, his voice echoing upward. "The man who drew up the plans for Senandaga followed the star-shaped design made famous by Marshall Sebastian de Vauban, military engineer for Louis XIV. Genius—sheer genius!" he added as they came to a wide-angled turn in the towering wall. "A century later my ancestor was imprisoned here."

Frank and Joe marvelled at the imposing defence the fort must have provided. "How could any army capture a place like Senandaga?" Joe asked.

"Not without much bloodshed," the millionaire

acknowledged. "A man like Vauban could have succeeded, though. Long before Chambord built Senandaga, Vauban devised a parallel trench system for assaulting forts." He explained how attacking armies in Europe had got nearer and nearer to fort walls by digging one parallel trench, then zigzagging ahead to dig another, and so on.

"Boy, what terrific strategy!" Frank said.

"Brilliant—brilliant," Mr Davenport agreed. "The Marquis de Chambord, by the way, was a great admirer of Vauban's achievements."

Chet glanced out at the peaceful lake, which once was the scene of warring canoes or attacking fleets. "It doesn't *seem* haunted," he whispered to the Hardys.

Frank was about to answer when a rumbling sound came from above. Looking up, he cried out:

"Watch out! The wall!"

A huge section of crumbling grey masonry collapsed in a cloud of dust and came toppling down.

·6·

Chet v. Impasto

THE crumbling wall broke into a spreading, plunging landslide.

"Quick!" Frank shouted.

Instantly he pulled Mr Davenport to safety while the others leaped from the path of the rocky avalanche.

When the danger was past, Frank saw that Mr Davenport was holding his hand to his chest and breathing hard. "Are you all right, sir?"

The art patron shook his head but said nothing. His face was pale and he hung on to the boy for support. Frank turned to the others. "I think we'd better get him to a doctor!"

They quickly returned to the car. Alex drove them immediately to Mr Davenport's physician in Cedartown. To everyone's relief, an examination showed that there was nothing seriously wrong.

"Just see that you get plenty of rest," the young doctor directed, "and stay away from dangerous ruins!"

As the limousine headed back to Millwood, the millionaire, looking somewhat better, pursed his lips and grumbled. "No sooner get to visit my own fort than it has to fall down on me. I can't understand it—Senandaga rock's not likely to give way like that."

48

Joe and Frank shared a frightening thought: Had the masonry been *pushed* down?

"You take care of yourself, Mr Davenport." Joe smiled. "Frank, Chet, and I are up here to earn our keep as detectives. We'll investigate the fort and keep you posted."

All three boys were eager for a second crack at Senandaga. Was a gold chain made by order of the Marquis de Chambord hidden somewhere beneath its ruins? If so, would they be able to beat the thief, or thieves, in finding the Prisoner-Painter's clue?

During a late lunch the boys asked Uncle Jim about Chauncey Gilman, the man for whom Mr Davenport apparently had a violent dislike.

"Gilman lives across the lake," he replied. "He's wealthy—inherited a lot—and is an art critic. Writes a column for the local paper."

Uncle Jim also explained that Gilman had bought a fort painting years ago from the Millwood philanthropist. "Mr Davenport has regretted it ever since."

He explained that the critic, a failure as an artist himself, had grown extremely harsh in his published statements about the school. "He's not a very pleasant fellow," Uncle Jim added. "You'll probably run into him here on Senandaga Day."

When they had finished eating, the Hardys called the local police and learned that the stolen car used by the antique-shop thief had been found abandoned off a highway outside Cedartown. "Maybe he's gone into hiding nearby," Frank conjectured. "We'll have to keep a sharp lookout."

The boys went to tell Mr Davenport about the theft. He was disturbed to learn of the stolen frame. "If

I'd known it was at the shop, I would've bought it," he fumed.

The art patron then opened a small safe and took out a photostat. It was a copy of an old, detailed map of Fort Senandaga, labelled in script, which Mr Davenport said the boys could borrow.

"This should be a big help when we begin combing the ruins for some clue to the treasure," said Frank, pocketing the map.

At Chet's urging, the Hardys agreed to attend a studio oil-painting class that afternoon. "You sleuths can still keep your eyes open," said the plump youth.

Joe eyed him suspiciously. "Chet Morton, I sense you've got an ulterior motive."

Chet grinned widely, but said nothing.

Uncle Jim welcomed the three boys to the cool, stone-walled room in which the class was held. Here, long, high windows let in ample daylight.

"I'll just watch," said Frank.

"Me too." Joe grinned. "We'll leave the brush-work to Chet."

The stout boy obtained an easel and the necessary art material, and chose a spot at the back of the room.

Ronnie Rush stood at an easel in front of Chet. He turned round and smirked. "You have talent?"

"I'll soon find out," Chet replied as the Hardys strolled over.

On impulse Joe asked, "Say, Ronnie, you use much of that alizarin crimson?"

Ronnie looked surprised. "Sure. Everybody does."

"In painting, that is?" Joe asked pointedly.

Ronnie stared in bewilderment. "Of course. Why?"

"Oh, just curious."

Jim Kenyon now came over to show his nephew about blending colours and brush techniques.

When he had moved away, Frank murmured to his brother, "Ronnie didn't act like he had anything to do with that cartridge shell."

Joe nodded. "I'd still like to find out why he's so resentful."

The brothers looked at Chet. Their stout pal, completely engrossed, was wielding his brush with vigorous strokes. Joe chuckled. "Chet's really got the painting bug."

A little later the Hardys decided to take a closer look at the fort paintings and headed for the gallery. As they approached the building, footsteps came up behind them. The boys turned to face Ronnie Rush. "I'd like to see those fort pictures," he said petulantly.

The Hardys were nonplussed. Finally Frank said, "Mr Kenyon told us no students were allowed in the gallery now."

Joe added, "Do you have a special interest in forts? Senandaga, for instance?"

"Oh, just the painting techniques," Ronnie said hastily. "And why are *you* two so interested?"

"We're doing some research on the fort's history," Frank replied.

"Oh. History." Ronnie squinted. He did not seem inclined to leave, so the brothers gave up their plan for the moment and returned to the studio where Chet was still working at his easel.

"Can we see your masterpiece?" Joe asked, grinning.

"Oh, no, fellows," Chet replied earnestly, waving them off. "Not yet."

After supper Frank said, "We ought to try another

tack. I vote we pay a visit to Mr Davenport's enemy."

Chet's eyes widened. "Chauncey Gilman?"

"Yes. After all, he owns a fort painting."

Joe was enthusiastic. "Maybe Gilman himself has information about the gold chain."

Taking Chet's jalopy, the three were soon heading north along the west shore of the lake, an area lined with summer homes. Farther on, imposing lakeside mansions came into view, and in another twenty minutes they pulled into a sloping gravel driveway. A chain-hung sign along the side read: CHAUNCEY GILMAN, ESQ. Atop the rise stood a handsome Tudor-style house overlooking the lake.

"What a setup!" Chet whistled as he parked.

From a shrubbed terrace at the rear, a plump, wavy-haired man rose from a lounge chair. He stared in disapproval at the vehicle and its smoking exhaust, then at the boys as they got out.

The three friends had never seen a man quite so elegantly attired. He wore a green velvet jacket, striped trousers, and white cravat.

"Are you sure you're at the right address?" he droned nasally, removing his glasses.

"Mr Gilman?" Frank enquired.

"The same."

Frank introduced himself and the others, explaining they were vacationing at Crown Lake and hoped to see his fort painting.

"Are you one of those *Millwood* students?" the critic asked disdainfully.

"Not exactly," Joe replied.

"Very well." Gilman shrugged and ushered the boys across the terrace towards a back door.

"Real friendly type," Joe whispered to the others.

Inside, the critic led them through elaborately furnished rooms, then up winding stairs into a large hall. To one side was an arched doorway.

"My own lake-view dining room," he announced, leading them past a suit of armour and round a long table on which lay a large dictionary. On the far wall he gestured towards a painting.

The canvas, not in the original frame, showed a distant twilight view of Fort Senandaga, with a thorn apple tree in the foreground. The boys noticed that the scene had a three-dimensional effect.

"A rather good effort," Gilman intoned grudgingly. "Acquired from a most misguided man, I might add. Fine impasto, don't you think?"

"Er—exquisite," Chet replied, receiving amazed looks from both Hardys. He bit off a smile and wondered what "impasto" meant. "Sounds like a salad," he thought.

The critic turned to Frank and Joe. "No doubt," he went on condescendingly, "you'll want to see the general's other paintings at that so-called art school." He sniggered with relish. "I'll be paying my annual visit there to the students' exhibition, and pass judgement on the—er—works of those amateur juveniles—a most amusing task!"

Chet had edged over to the large dictionary. He would get one up on the Hardys, and at the same time not feel so stupid about "impasto."

Frank observed their stout friend from the corner of his eye, but made no move to give him away. Chet picked up the book and leafed through it, backing towards the window for better light.

Joe, meanwhile, could not resist asking Gilman, "Do *you* paint?"

The plump man looked out of the window, his hands behind his back. "I am, first and foremost, a critic," he declared haughtily, "and widely known by the elite of the artistic world. I—"

Crash!

The Hardys and Gilman jumped and wheeled about. On the floor lay the suit of armour. Standing over it was Chet, his face flaming red. "S-sorry," he stammered. "I backed right into it." Quickly he closed the dictionary and tried to hide it behind his back.

"Studying too hard?" Frank grinned as he helped to right the armour. "No damage, sir."

The critic raised his eyes to the ceiling. "My nerves!"

Chet sheepishly placed the dictionary on the table and joined the brothers as they studied the fort painting. "*Impasto*," muttered the plump boy, "is the thick application of pigment to a canvas or panel, for your information."

"Okay, professor." Joe chuckled.

They peered closely at the picture's surface, trying to detect some kind of telltale marks in the composition. From several strategic questions, the Hardys gathered that Gilman knew nothing of any clue to the *chaîne d'or*.

Finally, the critic coughed meaningfully. "If you don't mind," he said, "I *must* be getting to work on an important critique."

The boys, disappointed in the outcome of their mission, thanked the man and left.

"So that's Chauncey Gilman!" Joe said scornfully as they headed south on the lake road. "What a swell-

The suit of armour crashed to the floor.

head! And he sure has it in for Millwood. No wonder Mr Davenport doesn't like him."

"You said it!" Chet agreed, "Uncle Jim and his students must resent a character like that."

Frank appeared lost in thought. "I wish we could do more in getting to the bottom of this mystery. If only we knew what kind of clue to look for!"

"Do you think Gilman has any interest in the gold chain?" Chet asked.

Frank shrugged. "He didn't act like it—but you never know."

Joe's lip curled. "He's too busy dreaming up acid criticisms."

A mist hung over the lake now, the water below them seeming almost colourless through the trees. Up ahead at a bend in the road, Chet noticed an observation area offering a commanding view of the lake. The boys decided to pull over for a look.

"Maybe we can see the fort from here," Joe said. Chet parked on the wide shoulder and they got out.

A strong wind coursed up the slopes from the lake. Several homes were scattered along the opposite shore. The boys looked out to their right. Barely visible in the dusk was the jutting outline of one of Senandaga's walls. The Hardys again speculated on the collapse of the fort section that morning.

Suddenly Joe leaned forward and asked curiously, "What kind of craft is that?"

The others looked down and saw a small white barge, coupled to a green tugboat. They could dimly make out two metal strands coming from the front of the barge.

"Oh, that must be the cable ferry Uncle Jim mentioned," Chet recalled. "It takes cars and passengers across the lake." He glanced at his watch. "Let's go back," he said. "Supper was a long time ago!" The famished boy grinned and the brothers laughed.

They started for the car. Joe, who was last, abruptly stopped in his tracks. His ears strained to catch a distant sound.

"Fellows, wait! Hear that?"

They listened intently. Echoing down the lake from the ramparts came the ominous thump, thump, thump of a drum!

·7·

An Angry Sculptor

"LISTEN!" Joe urged, as Frank and Chet joined him apprehensively at the lookout.

"What is it?" Chet asked.

Joe held up his hand for silence and they listened intently. Frank leaned far out in the direction of the mist-shrouded fort. The only sound was that of the wind through the trees.

Joe explained as they got back in the car. "I'm positive it was drumbeats!" he said emphatically. "It was coming from—the fort!"

A cold chill raced up Chet's spine. He shuddered. "Y-you think Senandaga really is h-haunted?"

"It could have been the wind playing tricks," Frank speculated. "Personally, I think it was your stomach rumbling, Chet. Why didn't you tell us you were so hungry?"

The three broke into laughter, and drove back to Millwood, where they persuaded the kind-hearted cook to provide them with a snack.

The Hardys suggested they check the grounds before going to bed. The place seemed to be deserted. Joe happened to glance over towards the moonlit gallery and noticed something move in the shadows. A man was crouching at the locked door!

"Somebody's trying to get into the gallery!"

The boys broke into a run across the lawn, but the man jumped up and tore into the woods.

"Fan out!" Frank yelled to Joe and Chet.

Separating, they crashed through the brush in pursuit. In the darkness ahead, they could hear pounding footsteps.

"This way!" Joe yelled, heading left towards the sound of a breaking twig.

"Where? I can't see a thing!" Chet stumbled into a fallen tree and groaned before following a shadow to his left. "F-Frank—is that you?"

"Yes. Come on! Over here!"

Darting quickly from one tree trunk to the next, Frank plunged forward through bushes, then paused. Hearing a branch snap, he rushed ahead to the left.

"He must have headed to the right!" Joe's voice rang out.

Squinting for a glimpse of the prowler, Frank jumped over some rocks and darted through a clearing. As he sprinted into an adjoining wooded patch, he collided with someone and went sprawling on the ground.

"Joe—it's you!"

"Frank!"

Presently they saw Chet's chunky shadow approach. "Where did he go?" Chet panted, exhausted.

Kneeling and breathing heavily, they listened for a sign of the fugitive. But there was only silence throughout the woods.

"That guy's a phantom," said Chet, mopping his forehead.

"One thing is certain," Frank remarked. "He knows the area well. Probably somebody local."

"Wonder who he was," Joe said as they hurried towards the gallery. "He was tall—definitely not the thief we've already seen."

The boys found that the gallery padlock had been tampered with, and hastily summoned Chet's uncle.

"We didn't get a good look at the man," Frank reported, "but this is definite proof there's more than one person after the fort treasure."

He phoned headquarters, and soon an officer arrived on the scene. He dusted the door for prints, and made a search of the grounds near the gallery.

"No footprints," he reported. "Check with us in the morning."

Afterwards, the young sleuths and Uncle Jim got tools and worked by lantern light to reinforce the lock.

Frank and Joe also inserted a high-watt bulb into the unused socket over the door, then switched on the light. It was past midnight when they gathered up the tools.

Mr Kenyon wiped his brow. "This bright light may discourage intruders. This gallery wasn't designed to hold off thieves!"

Joe grinned. "I hope *we* are."

The next morning Chet was snoring contentedly when the Hardys finished dressing. Strong tugs at his legs awakened him.

"Come on," Joe urged. "Up and at 'em! You're four hours behind the birds!"

The heavy youth grumbled and burrowed deeper into his covers.

"Breakfast is ready!" Joe shouted.

Covers flew up and Chet landed squarely on the floor with two feet.

After eating, the trio went directly to the gallery. This time no one interfered. They found the remaining fort paintings were as varied in style as they were in views of the impressive fortress.

Several were painted as if from the middle of Crown Lake; others as if from a nearby mountain. Some were night scenes, others broad daylight. Green and brown colours stood out boldly, and lighting effects were worked with fine brush strokes upon the fort's stone ledges.

All the paintings were signed with an interlaced J and D.

"As I see it," Frank observed, "there's a choice of ways in which a painter could leave a clue on canvas."

"Or in the frame," Chet added.

Frank nodded. "But I think the paintings themselves are the best bet. The clue could be a tiny word in a corner or even a symbol. Or"—he pointed to one picture—"it might be where a figure is standing—this Union soldier for instance."

"Also," Joe interposed, "we should keep our eyes open for any unusual colour or brush stroke."

By noon they had found nothing definite, but all three had kept notes of possible clues. Back in their room, the boys placed tracing paper over the photostat of the Senandaga map and marked the places they wanted to check. Joe then locked the map in his suitcase and put the tracing paper in his pocket. After lunch the Hardys were impatient to begin exploring the fort, but Chet had a suggestion.

"Uncle Jim told me there's a new instructor in sculpture. He's French, and has definite views on Fort Senandaga. Maybe we should see this René Follette."

The Hardys agreed, although they strongly suspected their chum was trying to postpone another visit to the old fort. First, Frank phoned police headquarters. No trace of the thief or of last evening's prowler had turned up. The fingerprints had proved inconclusive.

The Bayporters headed for the sculpture studio. On the way, they passed Ronnie at his easel. Chet twirled his beret and sang out, "Getting ready for the exhibition?"

The student sneered. "I'm all set to take first prize. Half the kids here can't paint a barn door."

Chet glanced at the garish orange and purple circles on Ronnie's canvas. "Rush" was signed at the bottom in large flourishing letters.

"You wouldn't understand it." Ronnie guffawed, then said slyly, "I saw you three coming out of the gallery. Did you give up painting lessons?"

"Not me," Chet declared cheerfully.

"Ha! I suppose you're going to enter the exhibition."

Chet's face grew red. The Hardys winked at each other but said nothing. The young detectives moved on.

As they entered the sculpture workshop, the fresh smell of clay reached their nostrils. Colourful pottery and ceramic figures stood on high tables, as well as several in bronze. A stocky, red-faced man with snapping black eyes was darting among his students. About fifteen boys and girls were standing before long tables, working on both clay and metal sculptures.

When he saw Chet and the Hardys the instructor beamed. "Come in, come in!" He made a sweeping gesture of welcome. "You are new, *n'est ce pas?* I am René Follette."

The boys explained that they were visiting Millwood

as guests. "We're especially interested in Fort Senandaga," said Frank. "Could—"

"Ah! *Magnifique!*" the Frenchman broke in dramatically. "I shall tell you the story." The boys settled down at an empty table by a narrow open window. Follette removed a denim apron and joined them.

His first words were startling. "Senandaga! *Bah!* Fort du Lac is the real name!" He struck his chest. "It was built by a Frenchman—le Marquis de Chambord."

Intrigued by the peppery sculptor, the Hardys asked him about the battle said to have taken place during the French-Indian conflict. "Is it true the British conquered the fort?" Frank asked.

"*Jamais!* Never!" was the violent protest. Waving his hands, the Frenchman told how the British, under the command of Lord Craig, coming by boat down Crown Lake, had attacked the bastion. They had forced the French to flee, but apparently had not held the fort long, since Chambord's men had returned to drive out their foe.

"Chambord was a great man!" Follette exulted. "His men were the last seen on the ramparts of Fort du Lac—*not* the Englanders!" He pounded the table fiercely.

At that moment Joe glimpsed a flash of grey moving away from the window. He could not be sure, but assumed it was someone in an artist's smock. Had the person been listening, or just passing by?

Frank was asking René Follette about the gold boom chain ordered by Chambord.

"I believe it *was* made," the sculptor replied. His voice lowered. "I also believe it was stolen—by the Britishers. It is my intention," he added, "to find the truth. In my own way."

With that, the excitable Frenchman rose and resumed his instruction.

Outside, the boys looked at one another. Chet grinned. "Mr Follette is ready to fight that battle all over again," he said. "Think it's true about the French being the last holders of Senandaga?"

Frank chuckled. "Mr Davenport may know. Why don't we drop over and see him?"

"Let's take the map along," Joe said. "I'll go back for it and meet you outside the mansion." He headed across the grounds to the storage building. At the top of the stairwell inside, he heard a scrambling noise from below. Somebody was in their room!

Tensely, Joe swung down the winding metal steps and burst inside the open door. Too late he heard a sound behind him. A crashing blow descended on his head. The room reeling, Joe sank to the floor.

Treacherous Detour

REGAINING his senses, Joe found himself on his bed, looking up at the anxious faces of Frank and Chet. He sat up groggily, wincing as he touched his throbbing head.

"Ooo, who—scalped me?"

"The same person who stole our map of the fort," Frank said, handing his brother a cool gauze compress.

"The map!" Joe exclaimed. "Stolen!" He remembered hearing the rummaging noise before he was struck unconscious.

Frank pointed to their scattered clothing. "Somebody prised open our suitcases. Anyhow, the photostat's gone. Too bad we didn't come back sooner to find out why you didn't show up."

Joe insisted he felt well enough to accompany Frank and Chet to inform Mr Davenport.

"I hope this theft won't upset him too much," Chet said worriedly.

"If it wasn't the picture thief or whoever we saw at the gallery last night, I've got another guess," Joe proposed. "Ronnie Rush."

"Possibly." Frank's brow creased. "It would help to find out if he's only being nosy, or if he has a special interest in the gallery besides 'research.'"

They picked up Jim Kenyon at his studio and walked together to the mansion.

"Too bad," he said upon hearing the boys' story. "As far as I know, Ronnie's background is okay. But I'll try to keep a closer watch on him."

They trudged up the drive and came upon Alex, now in overalls, weeding a flower border. Even in working clothes, the man had a formal manner. He nodded slightly to the boys as they passed.

Inside, the Hardys and their companions found the elderly Southerner in his study, moodily poking his cane at the toy fort. He brightened at the entrance of his visitors.

"I declare, I'm delighted to see you all. My fort problem's getting me down. Any progress on the treasure?"

Frank took a deep breath. "I'm afraid we have another theft to report."

Mr Davenport was greatly agitated after hearing of Joe's experience. "Bad business," he muttered. "Don't like any of you boys getting hurt."

Joe smilingly reassured him, "We're rugged. I'm sorry about the map, though."

"Have one other copy tucked away." Mr Davenport extracted a photostat from his safe and handed it to Frank.

"We'd like to visit the fort again," Frank said.

"Go right ahead. I don't mind *you* boys being there, so long as the confounded pub—"

Joe broke in hastily to ask about the strange drumbeats. Mr Davenport was intrigued, but had never heard the sounds.

Frank then asked about the sculptor's claim that

French soldiers had been the last to leave the fort in the disputed battle.

The elderly man gave a little smile. "My feeling is, boys, that there's truth on both sides. Trouble is, both Lord Craig and Chambord lost their lives at a battle just after Senandaga. There are questions no one may ever be able to answer."

Chet spoke up. "We've studied the pictures some more. We even visited Chauncey Gilman—oh!"

The forbidden name was out of Chet's mouth before he realized it! Mr Davenport began thumping his cane on a tea table, jarring the china.

"Gilman!" his voice rose. "Gilman! That long-nosed, uppity Yankee! If that stuffed-shirt critic's trying to lay his hands on more of my fort paintings—or the treasure—Why, I'll—"

Chet's uncle quickly eased the breathless art patron into a chair while Frank said soothingly, "Mr Davenport, we understand how you feel. But as detectives we have to investigate every lead. Mr Gilman isn't very likable, but I don't think he's a thief."

The old man gradually calmed down, and wiping his brow, apologized for his outburst. He gave Joe a key to the fort gate and a short while later the boys departed.

Outside, Joe said eagerly, "I'm for a trip to the fort, pronto."

Chet looked unhappy. "You go, fellows. I—er—have some work to do."

"Work!" Joe echoed teasingly.

Uncle Jim grinned. "Chet has promised to help spruce up the grounds for our exhibition. My students are devoting all their time to finishing their entries."

Joe grinned. "We'll pitch in and give you a hand

if you'll drive us to Senandaga. Is it a bargain, Chet?"

"Okay, okay!"

While Jim went off to a class, the Bayporters set to work. Chet and Joe teamed up to wash windows. Frank mowed the grass, starting with the area round the gallery.

Still wondering about the stolen fort map, he kept his eyes open for Ronnie. But the youth was nowhere to be seen.

Later, at the sculptor's studio, as the students were leaving, Frank found Joe washing the outside panes.

"This is one way to earn our keep." Frank grinned. "Say, where's Chet?"

"Don't know," Joe replied. "He and Uncle Jim went to the oil-painting studio about an hour ago. Let's check."

Joe put down his bucket and rags and the brothers walked over to the studio. Chet was perched atop a high, three-rung stool before an easel. He moved the brush slowly over his large canvas.

"Well," Joe said, laughing, "from window washer to artist. I should've known—from those fine rag strokes on certain windows."

Chet looked up. "I'm sorry, Joe," Chet said. "I'll do my share. But I just got so interested in—er—my painting. Besides, Uncle Jim thinks it's not bad."

"You know, Chet," Frank said, "I have a wild hunch your painting will turn up at the exhibition."

Somewhat embarrassed, Chet admitted this was his secret plan. The Hardys watched as their pal continued to work. When not biting the end of his paintbrush with indecision, he would hunch forward, dip the brush in a thick purple blob on his palette, and absorbedly make a squiggle on the canvas.

"What's it going to be?" Joe asked at last.

"You'll see," was all Chet said.

After a while the boys returned to their chores, and it was not until after supper that everything was finished.

The Hardys and Chet went down to the lake for a cooling dip before starting out for Senandaga. The afterglow of sunset cast the opposite shore in a pale-rose light. Dusk shrouded the wide lake. Frank was swimming some distance from shore when he heard a sound that made his spine tingle.

Like a distant heart-throb behind the promontory came the single beat of a drum, then silence, then the beat again!

"Fellows! Listen!" he shouted and swam over to Joe and Chet. They strained their ears.

"The drum!" Joe hissed.

The boys dashed out of the water. They found Uncle Jim and Mr Davenport talking near the mansion. Upon hearing the boys' report, both men agreed the young sleuths should investigate the fort at once, but cautioned them to be on guard.

"Not that I believe it is haunted, of course," added Mr Davenport. "But there could be some kind of danger lurking there."

The boys hurriedly dressed and drove off in the jalopy. Darkness was falling as they headed south. Chet switched on the headlights and guided the Queen round a series of curves until they reached the end of the lake. There were few houses, and only rarely a light. Chet slowed down.

The trees grew dense and overhung the road. From deep in the woods came the hoot of an owl, mournfully echoing over the constant whisper of cicadas. Like brittle fingers, branches clawed the side of the car.

"Willikers, it's spooky!" Chet said, rolling up his window. He turned right up a winding dirt road, then left.

Suddenly Chet screeched to a halt. The road was blocked by two wooden sawhorses! By the light of a flashing red lantern, the boys saw an arrowed white sign: DETOUR—LEFT—ROCKSLIDE.

"Guess we haven't much choice," Joe said. Chet turned the car and started down what proved to be an extremely narrow, steep lane.

The lake was visible below. Suddenly a tree loomed directly in their path. Hastily Chet yanked the wheel, but the car scraped against high rocks. As the Queen bounced over a yawning hole, Frank cried out:

"This isn't any detour! It's a trap!"

Panicky, Chet stamped on the brake. But the left front tyre had already pitched steeply down. Desperately he tried to swerve the rolling car.

"I can't stop!"

Faster and faster they skidded downwards. Like bulky phantoms, trees grazed the fenders as Chet steered frantically between them. Jolted, his hands lost control of the wheel.

"We're going into the lake!" Joe yelled.

The front of the car seemed to lurch into the air. Their heads banged the roof an instant before the Queen struck water. She stopped almost instantly.

Frank shouldered his door open and sloshed through the shallow depths to pull Chet out. Joe crawled from the back window and the three waded to shore.

"Everybody all right?" Frank asked breathlessly.

"Yes—but the Queen!" Chet exclaimed in dismay. The jalopy stood bumper-deep in the water.

Joe scrambled above to get help. Frank and Chet, grabbing a rope out of the trunk, moored the car to two trees to keep it from rolling out into the lake. There were dents and a smashed headlight, but the boys were worried there might be serious mechanical damage.

Chet heaved a sigh. "My poor Queen!"

Shivering in wet clothing, the two boys waited in the darkness for what seemed hours. Then they heard vehicles stopping and excited voices. Soon Joe appeared, accompanied by two policemen.

"I finally flagged down a car," he panted. The driver had notified the police, who in turn summoned a tow truck.

Joe had already given a report to the officers. "A nasty trick—that fake detour," one said. "We'll step up our patrol along there."

The boys wanted to stay until Chet's car was pulled to safety, but the policemen insisted on driving them back to Millwood.

Huddled under blankets, the three sleuths speculated among themselves on the return trip. Who could have set the dangerous trap? And why?

"I'll bet someone rigged it to keep us from Fort Senandaga!" Joe exclaimed.

"How'd he know we were going?"

"Could've overheard us talking about it," said Frank. "Maybe those drumbeats were to lure us there."

At the Millwood entrance they thanked the officers

and headed quickly towards their quarters. "Wait until Uncle Jim hears about this!" Chet's teeth chattered.

As they cut across the wide lawn, Joe glanced over at the grove in which the gallery stood. It was in total blackness.

"Funny," he murmured. "What happened to the light we put over the—?"

Instinctively sensing trouble, the Hardys streaked across the lawn. Chet followed. They found the front door unlocked and cautiously pushed it open.

A torch beam struck them squarely in the eyes! A shadowy figure approached. The boys dashed in, ready for a fight. The next moment they stopped short.

"Uncle Jim!" Chet gasped. "What—?"

The instructor's face was ashen. Wordlessly he flicked on the light switch and pointed towards the far wall of the room. *The twelve fort paintings were gone!*

·9·

The Hermit's Story

"ALL the Senandaga paintings—stolen!" Jim Kenyon's words echoed dismally across the stone gallery as the boys rushed over. The wall showed twelve empty picture hooks.

Uncle Jim told them he had returned from Cedartown a short while ago. He had gone to check the gallery, found that the bulb had been smashed, and a moment later, discovered the theft. "I was about to phone the police, then break the news to Mr Davenport."

"But how did the thief get in?" Joe asked.

The instructor pointed upwards. "The skylight."

The boys noticed a large section of panes was missing where the glassed roof met a wall.

"The thief must have had a lookout," Frank surmised, "while he was cutting the panes."

The police were called and arrived shortly to examine the gallery. They found the missing glass panes, but there were no fingerprints. Nothing of significance was discovered. When the officers had left, Jim and the boys went to the mansion.

It took them a long while to persuade Mr Davenport that the twelve paintings actually had been stolen. The art patron kept shaking his head, as if in a daze.

"What are we to do?" he lamented. "The thieves are still at large and growing bolder—Jason's paintings in their possession, and likely, the clue to Chambord's gold chain."

Suddenly he and Uncle Jim became aware of the boys' dishevelled appearance. "What on earth happened to you?" asked the instructor.

In the excitement, the Hardys and Chet had temporarily forgotten their own experiences. Quickly they described the ill-fated drive.

The two men listened in great astonishment and concern. Mr Davenport snapped out of his gloom. "Desperadoes!" he stormed. "Why, you boys could've been hurt something dreadful!"

"They're desperate all right," said Frank. "Which means they may tip their hand soon and give themselves away. The trouble is," he added, "somebody in the area seems to know every move we make, or are going to make."

"Do you think," asked Uncle Jim, "those drumbeats and your accident are related to the painting thefts?"

"Yes," replied Frank. "Whoever the mastermind is, he doesn't want us at Fort Senandaga to look for the gold chain."

Joe set his jaw. "We'll get there yet and do some hunting."

The weary boys slept late the next morning. After breakfast Chet phoned the Cedartown police. His jalopy had been salvaged, but it would take at least a week for repairs.

Chet groaned. "How will the Queen live without me?"

"Cheer up!" Joe grinned. "You're going to be pretty busy painting from now on. We're expecting big things from you at the exhibition!"

Chet slapped his forehead. "You're right! I've only got a little more than two days!" He pulled his beret from a pocket and pulled it on. "This calls for painting genius!"

"In the meantime," Joe said seriously, "we're stymied for transportation."

"Not quite," Frank replied. "We'll use one of the canoes."

"Great!" said Joe. "What's the first stop?"

"Turtle Island." Frank proposed that they visit the English hermit and have a look at his fort painting.

Chet wanted to go with his friends, but finally decided to work on his painting. The trio were about to separate when they saw Ronnie Rush setting up his easel near the main path.

At once the Bayporters hurried over. Joe asked bluntly, "Ronnie, we're missing a photostat of an old map. Have you seen it around?"

The student bit his lip. "Map? Why ask me? If I had, it'd be my business anyway."

"This one happens to be our business," Joe retorted. "You seem to be pretty good at spying. Maybe you saw the person who knocked me out, broke into our luggage, and stole the map."

Ronnie's face reddened, but he merely blustered, "I—I didn't see anybody. What's so special about an old map?"

"It's of Fort Senandaga," Joe said.

Ronnie gave a perceptible start, but at once took

up his palette and brush. "Stop bothering me. I've got to finish my picture."

"Your prize-winning one?" Chet asked airily.

"A lot you know about art, fatso!" Ronnie muttered.

The three boys turned away. "I'll show him," Chet vowed.

Joe grinned. "The brush is mightier than the sword!"

"Anyhow," Frank said, "we got a rise out of Ronnie about the map, though we still can't be sure he took it."

"Yes," Joe said, "but he sure didn't like our questions."

The Hardys got directions to Turtle Island from Uncle Jim, and permission to use his own canoe, then hurried to the boathouse. They lifted the handsome red wooden craft from its berth into the water. Joe settled himself in the bow, and Frank in the stern, then they paddled off.

Bright white sails were visible farther down the lake as they glided across the sun-speckled water. Here and there a motorboat sped along. The canoe traced a shimmering line over the surface as Frank steered towards a group of small islands a mile out.

"There's Turtle Island," Joe said presently, spotting a wooded hump of land straight ahead where a cabin of stone and log was partially visible.

Coasting between two large, jutting rocks, Frank steered the canoe on to a sandy strip. Nearby lay a weatherbeaten rowing boat. Joe jumped out and pulled in their craft. Suddenly they heard a ferocious barking, there was a flurry in the bushes, and a huge German shepherd dog appeared.

"Look out!" Frank cried.

The dog bared its teeth threateningly. Growling, it

crouched as if to spring. The Hardys darted backwards.

"Basker!" shouted a deep voice. "Hold, boy!"

The dog subsided instantly as a tall, sunburned man in a brown tweed suit emerged from the brush. Frank and Joe relaxed as he stroked the panting animal. The tall man peered at them beneath bushy eyebrows and greeted them in an English accent.

"Hello there!" he said cordially. "Terribly sorry about Basker—he's not used to seeing many people out here." He extended his hand. "Lloyd Everett's my name."

The boys introduced themselves, thinking Everett unusually well-dressed for a hermit. They told him why they had come. He agreed to let the Hardys inspect his Prisoner-Painter picture and led them towards the cabin.

"Dare say you chaps have had wind of that French gold-chain legend," he remarked. "I don't take any stock in it myself—it's false, like most of the past French claims about Fort Royal."

"Fort Royal?" Joe repeated.

Everett nodded. "Senandaga is its Indian name, but it's properly called Fort Royal, named by its last holder during the French-English campaigns, the great Lord Craig, my ancestor."

Remembering the French sculptor's account of the fort, Frank glanced at Joe.

In the simply furnished but comfortable living room, Everett lifted down the painting from its place over the fireplace. Frank took out a pocket magnifying glass and studied it closely. The view was painted as if from below the ramparts at Crown Lake's edge.

"A fine rendition," the Englishman remarked. "I

don't generally collect art, but since I'm interested in the historical aspects of Fort Royal, I persuaded Mr Davenport to sell it to me a few years back."

While Joe scrutinized the picture, Frank asked if it were true that French soldiers had been the last on the fort's ramparts.

"Nonsense! Sheer nonsense! Who told you that?" Everett demanded.

When Frank mentioned the Millwood sculptor, the hermit exclaimed, "Blast it! A Frenchman! What else?" Striding angrily over to a small cork board, he plucked out seven darts. In rapid order he pitched them at the board.

"This Follette told you a pack of lies about Chambord, no doubt," Everett growled. He did not pause for a response and proceeded to relate how Lord Craig had taken Senandaga. The French had apparently mismanaged their cannon defence and fled before Craig's forces.

When Joe mentioned the story of the English having stolen the *chaîne d'or*, Everett angrily plucked the darts from the board.

"As a descendant of Lord Craig, I shall not tolerate such lies. Here!" He handed the boys a small book. Its title was *The True Story of Fort Royal*. "Read this—you may keep it," he said. "I wrote the book myself when I first moved here to my island retreat."

The Hardys thanked him, intrigued by the differing accounts of the battle. The boys studied the Senandaga painting again. Suddenly Frank noticed a slight irregularity in a corner brush stroke.

"Joe, let me have the magnifier!"

Excited, he held the glass over the area. But he

looked up in disappointment. "It's just a scratch," he reported.

Nothing else unusual was detected in the painting. The brothers made a note of the location of two soldiers standing below the ramparts. They thanked the Englishman as he walked with them to the canoe.

"Wish you boys luck, of course," said Everett. "Take my advice—the so-called *chaîne d'or* doesn't exist. Just another of many French exaggerations." He added that he rarely crossed to the mainland except to buy provisions. He had not left the island in a month.

The Hardys waved as they pushed off. "Cheerio!" called Everett. "Be sure to read my book!"

Joe was dejected. "That painting was another lost hope. I guess all we can do now is search the fort itself for the chain. If there is one!"

"We also have the job of tracking down the thieves and stolen pictures," Frank said. "By the way, Everett told us he hadn't been off the island for a month. But his rowing boat was wet and muddy—and it hasn't rained for days!"

Joe remembered seeing oars in the boat also. Was the recluse lying? Did he know anything about the Millwood thefts?

"Well," Joe quipped, "we could always take a new case: Who *were* the last holders of Fort Senandaga—I mean, Fort Royal!"

"Or Fort du Lac!" Frank smiled, shifting his paddle to the right.

Smoothly, the brothers stroked forward. They were halfway to shore when Joe first noticed water round his feet.

"Frank! We're taking in water!"

Shipping his paddle, Joe slid back carefully to locate the leak. "I can't find it!" he cried out.

Frank quickly pulled in his paddle and crept forward. But he had no sooner taken a step than he heard a cracking noise.

"Joe—this wood—"

With a splintering noise, the section of flooring beneath Frank's left foot gave way, trapping his leg. Water poured in as the sinking canoe capsized.

The lake surface closed over the Hardys!

· 10 ·

Mysterious Flag

COLD stinging water coursed through Joe's mouth and nose as he sank beneath the surface. He could see the shadow of the capsized canoe above.

Shooting up for air, he immediately plunged beneath again.

With a mighty yank he freed Frank's leg from the hull, and both boys were soon hugging the splintered boat.

"Are—are you all right?" Joe gasped.

Frank coughed for several moments before answering. "Yes, except my leg's a bit sore. I don't get it, Joe. This canoe is practically new."

As the Hardys signalled an approaching motorboat, Joe noticed something on the canoe's hull. "Frank, look!"

Joe pointed to the jagged hole where Frank's leg had gone through, then at several smaller holes edged with a painted paste.

"This canoe was sabotaged!" he panted, treading water. "Somebody must have cut these holes, then used a sealer and paint! Whoever did it knew that it would just be a matter of time before water—or we—went through."

The motorboat, manned by a man and his wife,

pulled abreast of the stranded sleuths and helped them aboard. With the canoe in tow, they were soon on their way back to Millwood. Frank pulled a wet book from the pocket of his slacks.

The True Story of Fort Royal was soaked but safe!

At the school dock the Hardys thanked their rescuers and hurried across the grass. Several students eyed the water-soaked boys curiously. Chet and his uncle spotted them and came rushing up. They were mystified and worried upon hearing of the boat incident.

"Somebody must have been hoping you'd use my canoe," the instructor said grimly.

"You mean the trap was intended for Frank and Joe," Chet finished. "And maybe me too. No place is safe round here!"

As the Hardys changed into dry clothes they told of their visit to Lloyd Everett. Uncle Jim grinned. "He takes that battle as seriously as René Follette and Mr Davenport."

"And how!" Frank looked thoughtful. "He's friendly enough—doesn't look or act much like a hermit."

During a late lunch the three boys and Uncle Jim discussed possible suspects in the canoe episode. Ronnie Rush? The short thief? The gallery prowler?

Joe noticed that Chet was staring into space and said, "You decided what your picture's about?"

Chet grinned good-naturedly. "Okay, mind reader, I have. But you'll have to wait and see."

"Is your entry a still life, Chet?" Frank asked.

"Yes. A moving still life!"

The others groaned at the pun.

They were just leaving the kitchen when the art

patron stormed out of his study, swinging his cane. A magazine was clutched in his hand.

"Confound him! That fogbound, silky-voiced, boiled shirt! That honey-dewed melonhead—"

"Now what?" murmured Chet.

Mr Davenport was finally persuaded to calm down and explain. "Just look at this!" he directed, opening the magazine and pointing to a paragraph which read:

"In the coming days, it will be my consummate pleasure to review the Millwood Art Exhibition, the annual artistic joke of the region. The public would better spend its time at nearby Fort Senandaga than risk dying of laughter at the 'wood' painted at the Davenport 'mill.'"

Frank looked up in disgust. "This was written by Chauncey Gilman."

Mr Davenport said that the critic himself had sent him the magazine. As soon as possible the Hardys changed the subject. The boys told the patron of their unsuccessful study of Everett's fort painting, then of the canoe incident.

The Southerner, who had been tapping his cane rapidly on the floor, suddenly stopped. To the others' amazement, he announced, "There's one more painting. It's in my attic."

"What?" cried Joe.

"I declare, it slipped my mind," said the art patron. "Guess because it's the one work by Jason I never did like. Style's different from all the others, so I just plumb hid it."

"May we see it?" Frank asked quickly.

"Might as well." Mr Davenport led the excited group to the third floor and into a dim alcove. There he removed a dust-covered canvas from a cupboard and set it on an antique table. The boys studied it closely with the magnifier.

"This is a contrast to the other fort paintings," Frank remarked. "It's all done in blacks, greys, and pale yellows. The storm clouds over the fort are ghost-like."

"Indeed they are," said Mr. Davenport. "I don't know what got into Jason."

Frank examined the back of the picture. He pointed to one corner, where a faded date was scrawled in a wavering hand: April 1, 1865.

"That was just before the Civil War ended," said Uncle Jim.

Again the boys scrutinized the gloomy scene. The artist's initials were as usual in the lower corner, but were fainter than in the other paintings. Frank's mind was racing. Why had the Prisoner-Painter changed to such a sombre style?

Just then Mr Davenport looked at his watch. "I'm afraid you'll have to excuse me," he said. "Expecting the carpenter any minute. He's working on a project for me." A mischievous twinkle came into the man's eyes, and as they went downstairs, he chuckled softly. His visitors were curious, but he offered no explanation.

"Let's try the fort again," urged Joe. "Right now."

The Millwood owner insisted they borrow his limousine. "Alex isn't here today, so I won't need it." He handed them the car keys.

Outside, Uncle Jim excused himself to return to his students. Chet decided to stick with his painting. "I'll keep an eye on Ronnie Rush," he promised.

The fort map in Joe's pocket, the brothers headed

for the mansion garage. On the way, they passed a tall,
bearded man at an easel set up on a knoll. The Hardys
recognized Myles Warren, who ran the Cedar Sports
Shop.

"Hi," said Joe. "You must be one of the weekend
painters, only this is Wednesday."

"Yes," the man said pleasantly. "I'm rushing to
finish my picture for the exhibition."

The Hardys glanced at the canvas—a landscape
in vivid greens, reds, and yellow. Warren kept his
brush moving. "Tried that fishing at the north end yet?"

"No." Frank smiled. "We'll keep it in mind."

In the garage Frank slid behind the wheel of the
luxurious limousine and pulled out into the road above
Millwood.

It was late afternoon by the time they reached the
fort. There had been no trace of the fake detour sign.
Frank parked, and they unlocked the gate, then
climbed the hill towards the ramparts. Pausing on
the glacis, the boys looked at the map, then at the
tracing showing the locations of figures in the pictures.

The actual shape of Senandaga was that of a square
with diamond-shaped bastions at the corners of its
four ramparts.

Frank pointed to a high, wedge-shaped defensive
stonework which stood in front of the ditch. "That
must be the demilune—the south one. There's another
to the west."

They decided to begin their hunt by checking
outside the fort walls and ditch. First, the Hardys
walked north along the zigzagging ditch, then to the
spot where the wall had fallen. They stopped to examine
the rubble.

"Hey!" Joe yelled, pushing aside a rock. Underneath lay a round black object. "An old cannon ball!"

The Hardys wondered: Had it been hurled against the ancient wall to cause the collapse? They surveyed the crenellated walls of blocked stone. Although its soldiers and cannon were long gone, a forbidding, ominous silence seemed to make itself felt round the bastion.

As Frank's eyes passed over the crumbled roofs visible above the walls, he stopped suddenly. "Joe, look!"

Waving atop a flagpole on the southeast rampart was a white and gold flag!

"It's the flag used by the French before their revolution!" Frank exclaimed, recognizing the pattern of three white lilies. "But it wasn't here the first time we came."

"One thing is sure—it's no relic," Joe said. "Mr Davenport didn't mention anything about a flag."

They stared at the mysterious banner, recalling the drumbeats they had heard earlier. Who had placed the old French colours over the fort?

Hastily the Hardys continued along the ditch to an area which they had marked on their tracing sheet. They hoped to find some kind of marking or rock formation at the same spots the figures stood in the paintings.

"Over here, a little more to the right," Joe said, comparing the map and sheet. Frank noticed that freshly churned-up soil surrounded their feet.

"Joe! Somebody's been digging!"

"You're right!" Joe reached down and felt the earth.

"If the treasure was here," Frank reasoned, "we're out of luck."

They walked towards the west demilune. But halfway, Joe noticed a pillar of black smoke in the sky. It came from beyond a shadowed promontory to the north of the lake.

"Frank, that looks like a fire!"

"It is. I wonder—Joe! It's coming from Millwood!"

· 11 ·

The Lake Monster

"WE'VE got to get back!" Frank urged.

The brothers raced down the slope to the parked car and soon were streaking round the lake road leading to Millwood. The column of black smoke swirled higher and they heard sirens.

Reaching the school, Frank wheeled the limousine to the parking area and they jumped out.

"It's the boathouse!" Joe exclaimed.

Waves of intense heat rolled out from the flaming structure. The Hardys ran towards the lakeside, where a crowd watched the firemen fighting the holocaust.

The dock was already lost, and what had been canoes were smoking shells on the bank. Voices echoed as spumes of water played against the blazing boathouse. Suddenly Frank detected a strong oily smell in the air.

"Paraffin!" he said. "This fire must have been set!"

The Hardys spotted Uncle Jim and Chet among the spectators at the back of a cordoned-off area near a police car. Chet was glad to see his pals.

"Was anybody hurt?" Frank asked, worried.

"Fortunately, no," Mr Kenyon replied. "But our boat area is a complete ruin."

In an hour the fire had been extinguished. According

to a student, the conflagration had apparently broken out suddenly—on the lake itself.

"Which means somebody poured a paraffin slick on the water and ignited it," Frank said.

Chet nodded solemnly. "With the wind and floating pieces of burning wood, we're lucky it didn't spread along the whole shore front."

By now, most of the onlookers had dispersed and the fire engines and police car were leaving.

The Bayporters surveyed the grim, charred skeleton of the boathouse, wondering who the arsonist could have been, and what his motive was. Another attempt to discourage the Hardys from investigating Fort Senandaga?

"It wasn't Ronnie Rush who set it, anyway," Chet declared. "He was too busy making fun of my painting."

The three boys searched the burned wreckage for evidence. They found nothing but a fat, charred cork, smelling of paraffin, bobbing on the waterfront.

"A pretty slim clue," Joe muttered, stuffing the cork into his pocket. After supper they went with Uncle Jim to see Mr Davenport. He seemed inconsolable. The school's exhibition was only two days away, and the blackened ruins would detract greatly from the estate's appearance. Joe had an idea.

"We'll begin clearing away the debris first thing tomorrow, and have the lake front in good shape by Senandaga Day."

Mr Davenport brightened, and Uncle Jim said, "That would be a big help. At least the lake residents will be able to beach their boats."

"There's one person I suspect," the art patron burst

out angrily. "Who else would want to spoil our exhibition? A certain party down the lake."

The boys assumed he meant Chauncey Gilman, but somehow they could not picture the critic in the role of an arsonist.

The brothers then told the others about the mysterious French flag they had seen at the fort. Mr Davenport expressed complete bewilderment.

"A flag over Senandaga!" he exclaimed incredulously. "It must be the work of some stupid tourist! A trespasser!"

Frank doubted this, saying that even a practical joker might not go to the trouble of climbing the fence.

"Don't tell me a ghost put up that flag," Chet gulped.

Mr Davenport shook his head. "You can get to the fort by boat, too."

The Hardys left him, wondering if the strange incident was part of the puzzle they were trying to solve.

Directly after breakfast the boys plunged into the task of cleaning up the dock site. With axes and wheelbarrows, charred wood was cut up and carted away, as well as burned shrubbery. Up to their waists in water, Frank and Joe hewed down the remaining boathouse supports and dock stakes.

"Whew!" Chet exclaimed as noon approached. "I feel as though I'd been building a fort."

Ronnie Rush came up just then and looked on smugly. "Want to help?" Joe asked him.

"My time is too valuable," Ronnie said, and sauntered off.

"He may not have burned the docks, but he sure burns me up!" Chet muttered.

At last the boys finished their project, having set up bright buoys offshore. After lunch they were summoned to Cedartown Police Headquarters, where the chief handed them a photograph. "Recognize him?"

"The picture and frame thief!" Joe exclaimed.

"His name's Adrian Copler," the chief informed them, adding that the man had a long criminal record as a thief, especially of art objects. There was no indication of his being an arsonist.

"I wonder if he's the brains behind the thefts at Millwood," Frank said, "or if he's working for someone higher up."

The chief shrugged. "Copler seems to be as elusive as he is clever. But I'll keep men on the lookout."

Back at the school, the boys discussed their future trips to the fort. "The Queen's still laid up and we can't keep borrowing the limousine," said Frank. "A canoe would be fine—but the fire took care of that."

"Guess we'll have to rent a boat," Joe said.

When Mr Davenport heard of the boys' quandary, he called them into his study.

"We can't have you detectives grounded," he said. "How would you like to use a Colonial bateau?"

"A what?" Chet asked.

He smiled. "A bateau was a boat used during the French and Indian campaigns." Mr Davenport explained that the wooden craft, resembling a modern dory, had been used by the English as well as the French for carrying supplies and for scouting. The original bateaux were up to forty-five feet long; later, they varied in length.

"Sounds great!" Joe broke in. "But where can *we* get a bateau?"

"My carpenter, George Ashbach, has a keen interest in historical boats. Out of curiosity, he put together a bateau last year. Doesn't use it much, but I understand it's navigable. I'm sure he'd be glad to let you boys borrow it."

"Super!" Chet exclaimed.

The elderly Southerner beamed. "Mr Ashbach will be finishing up—my—er—job today. I'll talk to him."

"Are you building something?" Joe asked.

A devilish gleam sparkled in the patron's eyes. He smiled, but gave no answer.

That evening, as dusk fell, the boys sat on the bank, wondering whether they would hear the eerie drum-beats again.

"I'd like to know if that French flag was lowered at sundown," Joe commented.

"By the same ghost, maybe," Frank said, grinning.

Chet was not amused. "Aw, fellows!" He shivered. "Can't we talk about something—er—cheerful?"

The only sound was lapping water, ruffled by a chilly breeze. Chet glanced out over the lake to the greyish islands, huddled like waiting phantom ships. Dim lights were visible across the water, but to the south, where the fort lay, all was black.

Suddenly Chet stiffened. Out on the water, about fifty yards from where the boys sat, something broke the surface, then disappeared!

Rooted to his place, Chet blinked and looked again, his eyes as big as half dollars.

"What's the matter?" Joe asked. "Do you—?"

He broke off with a gasp as all three stared in disbelief.

A speck of white showed on the dark water. Then an immense, curved black shadow loomed larger and larger, gliding, waving towards them.

Chet stuttered with fear as the shadow drew near. It had a long neck and a huge glistening head, gaping jaws and long sharp teeth!

· 12 ·

A Strange Tomahawk

JUMPING up, Chet screamed, "A sea monster!"

In a burst of foam, the phantasmal creature sank beneath the surface and again emerged, its white eyes gleaming above moving jaws.

Frank and Joe dashed along the bank until they were abreast of the weird figure. It seemed at least thirty feet in length!

"It's a serpent!" Joe cried out.

They watched for the monster to surface. Then a subdued, drawling laugh broke the silence. Chet, terrified, had caught up with the brothers. The three stopped short as two figures emerged from the nearby woods.

"Mr Davenport!" Joe burst out, recognizing one of them.

"Frank! Joe! Chester!" The art patron grinned. "I reckon I must ask your forgiveness for being victimized by my Crown Lake monster!"

He introduced the tall, lean man with him as Mr Ashbach, the Cedartown carpenter.

"You mean that thing we just saw was *artificial*?" Joe asked.

The carpenter chuckled. "Joe," he said, "we had to test it on somebody, and we figured you young detectives were as tough a test as anybody."

95

Mr Davenport nodded. "Now you know what my building project is!"

Still mystified, the boys noticed wires in the men's hands trailing off into the water. They began reeling in and soon the "serpent" broke the surface. A minute later it lay on the shore. The boys walked round the huge object.

Shaped like a brontosaurus with gills, it had been built over a wood-and-wire frame. The "skin" was of inflated rubber, touched in spots with luminous paint. Both the neck and jaws were hinged, and the snouted head had been fitted with two light-bulb eyes and jagged rubber "teeth."

"It's ingenious!" Frank laughed.

"Thank you." The millionaire smiled, patting the wet rubber proudly.

Chet kicked a pebble, embarrassed. "Jiminy, do I feel like a goof! But what are you going to do with this—er—serpent, sir?"

"You boys will see, soon!"

The curious sleuths could learn no more about the redoubtable monster.

The Hardys arranged with Mr Ashbach to pick up the bateau at his shop the next day.

Later, walking back to their room, Chet was preoccupied with Mr Davenport's lake serpent. "I bet he's going to give rides on it!" Chet guessed finally.

Joe grinned. "Beats me."

After breakfast the next morning the Bayporters found the school grounds a beehive of activity. Uncle Jim and the students were busy getting the pictures in final shape for Saturday's exhibition.

Hurriedly the Hardys and Chet tidied up their

"A sea monster!" Chet screamed.

quarters. Frank's mind kept turning over an idea which had been growing steadily. "Maybe it's a wild one, but—" Suddenly he dashed from the room. "Come on, fellows!"

Mystified, Joe and Chet followed him across the grounds to the Davenport mansion. The door was open. Frank led the way upstairs to the musty attic alcove. Joe was excited. What inspiration had struck his brother so forcibly?

Frank lifted the fort painting carefully on to the table. Chet wore an expression of utter perplexity as Frank pointed to the date on the back of the canvas. "This was the last picture Jason Davenport did. I think that's why the style is so different—he knew he was going to die."

"I get it!" Joe exclaimed excitedly. "He must have left the clue in this picture, knowing that he'd never have a chance to get the treasure himself," Joe guessed.

"Right." Frank now indicated the specklike daubs on the canvas. "Let's study them from a distance."

Frank set the painting against an opposite wall. At first the boys noticed nothing unusual. Then they were starled to see, out of grey and yellowish dabs, a design taking shape in the corner!

It was a tomahawk, entwined by a chain!

"The treasure clue!" Chet whooped.

The image seemed to lose itself as they stepped closer, then to reappear when they stood back.

"There must be a similar marking somewhere inside the fort!" Joe exclaimed.

The boys then noticed that the tomahawk handle had small notches, and wondered what these meant.

"The main thing is to keep this a close secret," Frank cautioned.

When they showed Mr Davenport their discovery, he congratulated the boys heartily.

"It was Frank's brainstorm," Joe said.

The art patron looked at the painting. "I should have known Jason had a special reason for using that strange style."

The millionaire, too, was puzzled by the notched tomahawk.

"Did Indians fight at Senandaga?" Frank asked.

"They were involved in the Crown Lake campaigns," Davenport replied, "but it's not known whether they played a major role at the fort itself. I've studied the battle for years, but there always seems to be a piece missing."

The boys wondered if the chain-entwined tomahawk had any relation to the mysterious fort conflict?

"We've got to get inside Senandaga," Joe declared.

The boys hurried to tell Uncle Jim the good news, and of their plan to search the fort that evening. Chet then excused himself to work on his painting. The boys were about to part when the French sculptor came running over. He carried three pamphlets.

"*Bonjour!*" he cried. "I hear you will use a bateau. Wonderful! A fine boat it is, used by le Marquis de Chambord. Here, my friends, these are for you!"

He handed each boy a pamphlet. The title was *The Final French Victory at Fort du Lac.*

Follette pounded his chest proudly. "This I wrote to give the true account of this battle. Read it. *Au revoir!*"

Joe chuckled. "The second 'true' story of Senandaga."

After the Hardys left for Mr. Ashbach's shop, Chet worked feverishly on his painting, even forgetting to eat lunch. By midafternoon the chunky boy realized he was ravenous and went to the house for a snack.

As Chet came outside he heard a horn blare urgently. He looked up in astonishment. A car, with a trailer bouncing behind it, was pulling into the drive. On the trailer sat an unusual-looking grey boat, flat-bottomed and tapered at both ends.

The car stopped and Frank and Joe hopped out. As Chet hurried over, Joe grinned. "Behold the bateau!"

"You sure she's seaworthy?" Chet asked, cocking his head.

"Indeed she is," came a deep voice as the carpenter, Mr Ashbach, got out of the car.

He and the boys hauled the old-fashioned craft down to the lake and beached it a short distance from the water. The young detectives thanked Mr Ashbach who wished them luck and left.

Chet now studied the bateau curiously, noting its overlapping board construction. He asked about a pair of long poles lying in the bottom beside the paddles.

"The poles are used in shallow water," Frank explained.

As soon as dusk fell, the boys eagerly launched the bateau and clambered in. Jim Kenyon came to see them off. "Be careful," he warned. "Weather doesn't look good."

Heavy dark clouds shrouded the lake and the wind was rising, but the boys were undaunted. Chet was in the middle seat while Frank stood in the rear and Joe in the bow. Plying the poles, the Hardys got the Colonial craft under way.

"Wow, this is smooth!" Chet said. "How long is she?"

"Fifteen feet," Joe answered, "and four wide."

The brothers at first had trouble but soon were poling in rhythm. They were amazed at the ease with which the bateau could be moved.

With the strong wind at their backs, they passed several islands. The darkening sky remained overcast and few private boats were out. "Hope the rain holds off for Senandaga Day tomorrow," Chet said anxiously.

Joe grinned. "You can always put an umbrella over your painting."

Reaching depeer water, the Hardys switched to paddles. Presently they approached the cable-ferry dock on the west shore.

The passenger barge was just pulling out. There was only one car aboard. The boys could barely see the cables stretching taut, reaching into the water.

The wind was now lashing the lake into a mass of whitecaps.

"It won't be any picnic returning against this gale," Joe remarked, as they paddled abreast of the chugging ferry. Its tugboat pilot waved to them from the lighted cabin.

Suddenly they saw him spin the steering wheel frantically, then race out on to the passenger barge.

"Something's wrong!" Joe exclaimed. The three boys leaped to their feet. Frank looked back at the dock and saw two metal strands lying slack on the choppy surface!

"The cables have broken!" he cried out.

The pilot had dashed to the rear of the pitching barge. Suddenly he staggered in a terrific blast of wind and toppled overboard!

Horrified, the boys watched the ferry veer wildly off course!

· 13 ·

Detective Guides

THE ferry drifted aimlessly on the storm-tossed lake past the dock, while its pilot was struggling to keep afloat. Paddling strenuously, the Hardys swung about to the rescue.

Swiftly the bateau closed the gap. The ferry passengers, two women, huddled panic-stricken in their car.

"You fellows get the pilot!" Frank said, flipping his paddle to Chet. "I'm going for the boat."

In a flash he was overboard and swimming through choppy waves. Finally he managed to grasp the end of the ferry barge and pull himself aboard. Frank ran past the car, tore into the pilot's cabin of the tug, and spun the wheel hard to the left.

He realized cutting the motor would be dangerous, since the heavy craft would only drift farther. Determinedly, he steered against the strong current.

At first it seemed useless. Then, slowly, the ferry backed towards the cable area, where Frank swung her to the right and headed for the far dock.

Just before reaching it, Frank cut the engine. Three men quickly secured the ferry and raced into the pilot's cabin.

"Young fellow—we can't thank you enough!"

one of them said to Frank. "There could have been a tragic accident."

The women, shaken and pale, added their praise as they were helped ashore.

Frank peered worriedly out over the wind-driven water. To his relief he saw the bateau, with Joe and Chet paddling and the pilot safely aboard, ploughing crosscurrent. When they pulled in, all three boys were warmly congratulated.

"Your presence of mind saved us all!" the pilot said gratefully.

Trying to determine what had happened, two of the dockworkers began reeling in the cable sections attached to the pier.

"How could they have broken so suddenly?" Chet asked, as the ends of the cables came to view. To everyone's astonishment, there was no sign of fraying.

"The cables were cut!" Joe cried out.

The pilot and dockers agreed. They said that the ferry had run for years without a cable breakdown. "I'm afraid," said the pilot, "it'll be some time before we're able to repair the damage."

After local authorities had been notified, the pilot insisted on driving the boys back to Millwood. He located a boat trailer on which to tow the bateau.

During the trip they discussed the accident. Who could have cut the ferry cables? Was there any connection between this, the art thefts, and the other strange occurrences?

"It'll probably cut down the turnout at our exhibition tomorrow." Chet sighed gloomily.

"It sure didn't help our treasure search," Joe murmured.

Once back in their room, and after a hot shower, the boys felt less despondent. Frank suggested that he and Joe offer to act as guides at Senandaga. "It'll give us a chance to look round inside the fort," he added.

They consulted with Uncle Jim, who was shocked to learn of the ferry mishap. He readily agreed to the Hardys' proposal and was sure Mr Davenport would concur.

The exhausted sleuths then went to bed. "At least," thought Chet in satisfaction as he dozed off, "my painting is ready."

When Joe woke the next morning he hopped to the window. "The sun's out!" he exclaimed. "Wake up, fellows!"

After breakfast the Hardys wished Chet luck as he hurried off with his painting. The entire school grounds were devoted to the display. Some students hung their watercolours and oils on a long wooden backing sheltered by a red-striped awning. Other paintings stood on easels scattered about the lawn. The sculpture entries were displayed on several long benches near the judges' table.

Meanwhile, the Hardys were ready to tackle their job at the fort. They had decided to go in the bateau. Heading for the lake, they met Mr Davenport, dressed impeccably in a white summer suit. He was in good spirits.

"Happy Senandaga Day, boys!" he drawled. "Great idea you two being guides." Frowning slightly, he cautioned them to admit the tourists only in groups and to keep them at the ground level of the fort ruins.

"Safer that way," he said. "Also, less chance for

someone to sneak off alone and look for the treasure."

"We'll do our best," Frank promised.

Soon the brothers were paddling down-lake in the bateau. They passed several canoes and motorboats heading in the direction of Millwood. "Looks as if the ferry accident may not affect attendance too much," Joe said.

Rounding the promontory, the Hardys looked up at the flagpole over the sprawling grey fortress. They could not believe their eyes. A banner fluttered from the staff, but this one bore three crosses, in red, white and blue.

"It's the British Union Jack!" Frank exclaimed.

Quickly the boys poled into a cove at the foot of the fort and beached their craft. They scrambled up a steep path and made their way round to the moss-covered entrance passageway in the north wall.

The brothers hurried through it and found themselves on the old parade grounds. Round the sides stood the ruins of two barracks and the officers' quarters. In the centre was a deep hole which, according to their map, had once been a well. As a precaution, they placed some old planks over it.

The Hardys once more stared up at the British flag.

"Well," said Frank, "if there's a ghost prowling around Senandaga, now's the time to track him down. Visitors will be arriving soon."

They walked about the massive, crumbling interior. After circling the parapets, the boys reached the south demilune by a wooden drawbridge, which Mr Davenport had had reconstructed. After checking the west demilune, they headed back through the entrance tunnel.

"No flag-raising ghosts so far," Joe quipped as they walked inland to unlock the promontory gate.

"The ramparts seem safe enough," Frank observed, "but the west demilune, dungeons, and stores are in bad shape. They'll have to be off limits."

Soon a trickle of tourists began. Frank and Joe took turns meeting them at the gate and escorting them, careful to keep the visitors in groups. After a while the sightseers swelled in number. Several times the Hardys were asked about the ghost rumours, and also about the British flag. The brothers would grin, merely saying these were mysteries no one had yet solved.

Frank and Joe were kept so busy they had little opportunity to look for any tomahawk marking. At noon they hastily ate sandwiches they had brought, then resumed their job. Later, Jim Kenyon dropped in to see how they were faring.

"Business here is fine," Frank reported. "How is the exhibition doing—and Chet?"

"We have a good crowd. And my nephew's as happy as a lark. His painting has attracted a lot of attention." Uncle Jim left, reminding the Hardys that the judging would be at seven o'clock.

"We'll be there," Joe said.

During the afternoon the boys overheard some of the visitors commenting on the Millwood exhibition. One elderly lady said to her companion, "That still life by that Morton boy is striking!" The Hardys exchanged grins.

They found most people were impressed by the brooding majesty of the Senandaga ruins and several spoke in favour of the fort being restored.

Minutes before closing time, Frank led the last

tour round the fort. Suddenly, from the ramp, he noticed a boy of about six make a beeline for the fort well. Frank saw with horror that the boards no longer covered it, but had been shifted to one side!

"That's dangerous—stop!" he shouted, running down the ramp.

But the child ignored the warning and leaned far over the yawning hole. A cry broke from the boy's lips as he lost his balance. Frank just managed to yank him to safety. He patted the youngster's head reassuringly as the frightened mother dashed up.

"I'm sorry," Frank said. "We had these boards over the hole. They were moved."

The woman thanked Frank and quickly led her son away.

When the last visitor had left, the Hardys went over to the well. Each wondered the same thing: Had somebody moved the boards on purpose, hoping to cause an accident? If so, was it the work of the same enemy?

"I sure wish we could wait for sunset to see if anybody lowers that flag," said Joe.

"So do I. But we promised to be back. Chet will be disappointed if we don't show up."

It was now a little before six o'clock. They hurried down and set off in the bateau. Poling off, they looked back at Fort Senandaga. The Union Jack was still waving from the mast.

"I wonder," Frank said, "if these flags popping up have some connection with Senandaga Day—and that mysterious battle."

"Could be."

As soon as they had landed at the Millwood beach,

the Hardys sought out Chet among the throng of visitors and art students.

They spotted him under a tree, and were astonished to see Chet, looking dejected, lifting his canvas from the easel.

"Why so glum, pal?" Frank greeted him. "We heard you were a big hit!"

Chet's face grew longer. "It was swell until just this minute," he mumbled. "I went to get some lemonade. While I was gone—"

Unable to finish, Chet swallowed and held up his painting. Frank and Joe gasped. What had been a still life of purple grapes in a yellow basket was smeared with blobs of dripping, green paint!

· 14 ·

Lucky Watermelon

"My painting's ruined!" Chet looked sadly at the ugly blotches on the canvas.

"That's a dirty trick!" Joe said, as Frank looked round angrily for possible suspects.

"What about Ronnie Rush?" Joe asked. "I wouldn't put it past him, especially if he was jealous of the hit your painting made."

At the moment Ronnie was not in sight. Frank had an idea. "Chet! You've still got a little time before the judges arrive. Maybe you can fix up the picture."

Chet seemed doubtful, but Joe quickly joined in to raise his hopes. "Look—only the grapes in the centre are ruined—the rest is okay. You could make those green paint blobs into something else!"

"Maybe you're right!" — Chet acknowledged, brightening. "I'll try it!" Carrying his canvas, he trotted excitedly towards the painting studio.

"What a blow for Chet!" Frank commented.

Joe agreed. "He was really crushed."

The Hardys met Uncle Jim. His face fell when they told him of the prank, but he was reassured on hearing of Chet's last-minute attempt. "I'll run over and try to keep up his inspiration!"

The Hardys then saw Mr Davenport at the sheltered

exhibition area, and went over. The elderly patron was walking from one canvas to the next. He spoke volubly, proudly commending his students.

"Well constructed, Bob, good attack!" he told one smiling boy, and moved on to a large, historical battle scene done by another youth.

"Excellent subject, Cliff! You've got your figures well deployed!" Twirling his cane happily, he proceeded to another entry. Next to it, looking nervous, stood a blonde-haired girl. Her entry was an imaginative view of the Millwood mansion.

"Good thickness of paint there, Ellen." Mr Davenport beamed. "Invulnerably designed!"

Joe chuckled. "He sounds as if he's talking about the construction of a fort!"

Frank laughed, but quickly became grim. He pointed to a knoll some distance away.

Ronnie Rush stood on the slope near two easels. He had a garish painting displayed on each. The Hardys hurried up to him.

"Say, what happened to your fat friend?" he asked, smirking. "He get cold feet and withdraw from the exhibition?"

"Not yet," Frank said coldly. "Do you know who messed up Chet's painting?"

The smug look on Ronnie's face turned to one of anxiety but only for a moment. He sniggered. "Fatso probably messed it up himself." He pointed to his canvases. "The judges will know *good* stuff when they see it. Say," he added abruptly, "why are you two cruising round in that weird boat, anyhow?"

"Part of our research," Joe replied tersely. By now it was almost seven o'clock, and the Hardys wondered

how Chet was making out. They started for the studio
and met Chet coming out, his canvas grasped carefully
in both hands.

"Any luck?" Joe asked eagerly.

"I hope so." Chet held out his revised painting.

The yellow basket now contained a large, green,
elliptical fruit. Below was the title—"Still Life of a
Watermelon in a Basket."

Frank and Joe praised their friend's ingenuity. "It
looks good enough to eat, Chet!" Frank grinned.

For the next hour the four judges viewed the
paintings and sculptures, frequently jotting down
notes.

The Hardys diverted Chet somewhat by telling of
their experiences at the fort that day. The plump boy
grew tense, however, as the judges paused at his easel.
Inscrutably they eyed the still life, scribbled on their
pads, and passed on to the next painting. Chet shrugged.
"Guess I don't have a chance."

An air of anticipation hushed the crowd as the judges
returned to their table and conferred privately. Finally
they handed a sheet of paper to Jim Kenyon, who
announced:

"Ladies and gentlemen, we're ready to award the
prizes."

The crowd surged close, and waited silently. First,
the sculpture awards were read by René Follette.
Mr Davenport stood next to the prize table and
handed out a ribbon and a gift to the three winners.

Uncle Jim stepped forward to give the painting
awards.

"Boy, even I've got butterflies—they're coming
out of my ears!" Joe whispered.

"First prize for the best watercolour goes to 'Night Crossing' by Carol Allen."

Applause accompanied each announcement as the lucky students accepted a ribbon and a gift. A smile crossed the instructor's face.

"And finally, first prize for the most original work, in all categories, goes to 'Still Life of a Watermelon in a Basket' by Chester Morton!"

Chet was speechless with delighted surprise.

"Go ahead, pal!" the elated Hardys shouted above the applause, slapping their friend on the back.

Proudly Chet went forward to receive handshakes from both his uncle and Mr Davenport. Several students congratulated him warmly as he squeezed his way back to Frank and Joe.

"Look what I got—a complete oil-paint set!" He beamed, cradling a large wooden box in his arms. "Thanks a lot, fellows, for your encouragement."

Joe could not resist a pun. "We knew it'd just be a matter of time before something tickled your palette!"

The three Bayporters laughed.

"O-oh, look who's coming," Frank said as Ronnie Rush pushed through the crowd. His name had not been among the prize winners and his face showed it.

He glared resentfully at Chet. "Just plain dumb luck, fatso!" Ronnie kicked at a rock and marched angrily up the hill.

"What a poor loser!" Joe said.

"Maybe I should have thanked him," Chet said, "if he did try to make trouble for me."

"Speaking of trouble," Joe said tersely, "look at what's coming." He pointed to the lake where a cabin cruiser was anchored a little way beyond the promontory. Standing on deck was Chauncey Gilman! Then the pilot rowed him to the beach and helped Gilman step ashore.

The critic, as elegantly dressed as before, moved disdainfully through the throng. The Hardys and Chet watched as Uncle Jim greeted the newcomer guardedly. Mr Davenport followed, clearly exerting all his willpower to keep calm. "I trust, sir," he said in a formal manner, "you will be fair in your review."

"Fair?" Gilman repeated loftily. "Why, the only way I could be fair to your juveniles' exhibition would be to shut my eyes!"

With a shrill laugh, he moved away and began viewing the students' paintings. Mr Davenport, scowling, trailed behind, accompanied by Jim and the three boys. Gilman paused at the painting which had taken the first prize.

"My, my. If this is one of the best, what *must* the worst be!"

With apprehension, the boys watched Gilman proceed, audibly abusing the paintings and sculptures one after another.

"Tsk! Tsk! Who victimized *this* canvas?" He pointed at a landscape done in watercolour. The girl who had painted it seemed on the verge of tears.

When he came to Chet's still life, the reviewer burst into high-pitched laughter.

"Oh, priceless, priceless! The blue ribbon must be from a fruit market!"

Although annoyed, Chet was not greatly upset by Gilman's remark, and Uncle Jim said, "The judges thought the exhibition today was one of the finest they had ever seen. The worst thing," he added, "is that Gilman's derogatory comments about Mill-wood will be printed."

Mr Davenport had been unusually quiet. The boys noticed a peculiar expression on his face as Chauncey Gilman closed his notebook and said, "Thank you all for a most entertaining evening. Better luck next year!"

As Gilman strutted towards his boat, Mr Davenport whispered to Jim Kenyon. The instructor, looking puzzled, called for everyone's attention. "Mr Davenport wants us all to go right out to the promontory," Uncle Jim announced. "It's a surprise."

The group, sensing something unusual afoot, soon gathered at the end of the dusky headland. Gilman's boat could be seen approaching the lighted cruiser.

The Hardys and Chet were surprised to see Mr Ashbach crouched beneath them on the bank, and, at some distance to the right, Mr Davenport, also bending low. Each man held the end of a wire!

Gilman's droning laugh could be heard over the splash of the oars. Then, at a signal from the millionaire, Mr Ashbach began pulling his wire.

The next moment a luminous serpent's head with gleaming white teeth broke the surface just ahead of the rowing-boat! Writhing, it headed for the craft.

Gilman shot up out of his seat, giving a shriek of terror.

"A m-monster! It's—it's a monster! Rogers! Help! Rogers!" he blubbered. "Save me!"

· 15 ·

An Eerie Vigil

THE hideous serpent bumped violently into the rowing-boat. With howls of horror, Chauncey Gilman and his pilot were pitched overboard. They floundered wildly in the lake, and the soggy notebook sank out of sight.

As the glistening monster heaved out of the water towards them, Gilman and the boatman splashed furiously for the cabin cruiser.

The group gathered on the promontory rocked with laughter. Doubled up with mirth, the Hardys, Chet, and Uncle Jim saw a grinning Mr Davenport finally relax his wire, and the carpenter did the same.

"So the 'monster' was constructed just for Chauncey Gilman!" Joe said as the millionaire climbed up to join them.

"Yes, siree. And I'll see that he reads a detailed account—*in print*," declared Mr Davenport.

Happily, the group dispersed for the night. All the next day the Millwood grounds echoed with laughter at the successful serpent scare.

On Monday morning, as Frank hung up the phone in the mansion hallway, Joe asked, "Any word on Adrian Copler?"

"Not a thing," Frank reported. "The chief says

Copler's done a complete vanishing job. The police did find an unrusted hacksaw underwater near where the ferry cables were cut. They're following that clue."

Frank also had learned that a statewide check was being made on art dealers for the stolen fort paintings.

Chet, having just finished breakfast, joined the brothers. "Well," he said as they went outside, "what's for today?"

"A camp-out tonight," Joe said promptly.

"Great!" Chet responded. "Where?"

"Senandaga."

"S-Senandaga?" Chet gulped. "Of all places to pick!"

Frank grinned. "Chet, you may have a chance to paint some ghosts." He added seriously, "We've got to unearth that tomahawk clue before somebody else does."

"You're right."

The Bayporters went into Cedartown to buy food and other necessary supplies. Finding no hardware shop, they went to the sports shop. Myles Warren was not there, but a crew-cut youth waited on them. With difficulty, he finally located three folding-type spades.

"Sorry for the delay," he apologized. "Don't know the stock as well as Mr Warren."

"Is he on holiday?" Frank asked.

"No, but several days a week he goes out to do some painting. Can I get you anything else?"

The boys picked out three torches, sleeping bags, and a scout knife. "Guess that's all," Joe said.

"Where are you fellows going to camp?" asked the clerk.

"Probably down at the south end of the lake," Frank replied noncommittally.

The assistant shook his head. "You wouldn't catch me in that neck of the woods. From what I hear about that fort, I'd keep as far away as I could. But—good luck."

After informing Uncle Jim and Mr Davenport of their camping plan, the boys loaded up the bateau. Swiftly they pushed off and headed south. When the fort came into view, they glanced at the flagpole. The Union Jack was gone.

Joe stopped paddling. "That's weird," he said. "First French, then British, now none!"

"Whoever put them up," said Frank, "may come by boat. He'd have an easier time getting in than climbing the fence."

"By boat," Joe repeated.

The brothers exchanged glances. "You two have an idea," Chet said knowingly. "What is it?"

Frank reminded him of the wet rowing-boat on Turtle Island, which contradicted the hermit's claim that he had not left the island for a month. "He was mighty opposed to the French claims at Senandaga," Frank recalled. "And don't forget his true account of—Fort Royal. He might have raised the Union Jack."

The bateau was guided past protruding rocks, and into the cove. The boys landed and climbed up to the old fort.

"We might as well start on the outside," Frank suggested, referring to the map. "If you see anything resembling a tomahawk, let out a war whoop."

The boys split up, each taking a designated area of the stone perimeter. They moved slowly along the shallow ditch, inspecting the huge stone blocks as far up the wall as the eye could see.

The task seemed endless and tedious, but they could not afford to dismiss the possibility of finding clues lying outside the fort.

Several hours later Joe called to Chet, "Any luck?"

A fatigued voice echoed from round a bend in the wall. "No. I think I'm going to be counting stones in my sleep."

The young sleuths paused to eat a sandwich, then resumed their search. The afternoon sun grew hotter by the hour. Twice they took breaks at the lakeside, refreshing themselves from canteens.

"There must be a million square miles of stone in this fort." Chet sighed, cooling his bare feet in the water.

A little later first Joe, then Chet, came upon freshly dug and refilled holes outside the ditch.

"Someone else is still searching," Joe remarked.

Suddenly Chet glimpsed a figure watching them from the wooded shore below.

"Ronnie Rush!"

They started towards the student. He turned and disappeared into the woods.

"Snooping again," Joe said. "Maybe he dug these holes."

They decided not to waste time in pursuit—Ronnie had too much of a head start.

It was late afternoon before the boys had finished examining the wall sections still standing. No luck. There were piles of fallen masonry they had not even touched.

"It'll take us days to go through them," Frank said.

"I think tomorrow we should concentrate on the inside."

"Whew! I'm bushed—and empty!" Chet declared. "Let's pitch camp and cook up some grub."

The boys decided not to build their campfire near the fort. "No use advertising our presence," Joe said.

As they started down to the bateau, Frank's foot struck something metallic.

"Look!"

Reaching down, he picked up a wooden-handled, chisel-like tool. There were traces of clay on the blade, which was only slightly rusted.

"It's a sculpture knife!" Frank said, turning it over in his hand. He detected two letters scratched on the wood—R. F.

"The owner's initials."

"René Follette, the French sculptor!" Joe burst out. "I wonder what he was doing here!"

"And he believes in Chambord's gold chain," Chet put in. "Except he thinks the British took it. Wow! I'm mixed up!"

Frank said decisively, "We're going to have a talk with Mr Follette when we get back tomorrow."

Tired and hungry, they set off in the bateau. Reaching a point on the shore beyond the promontory, Joe spotted a small clearing inland. Quickly they tied up and soon had a fire going. The hungry boys thoroughly enjoyed a simple meal of frankfurters and beans. When the sun had dropped behind the western hills, they doused the fire and pushed off in the bateau.

A chilling wind rolled down the lake as they neared the fort, its massive, jagged hulk outlined against the night sky.

The Hardys paddled cautiously between the out-jutting rocks and pulled ashore. Carrying sleeping bags and torches, they crept up the slope.

Some fifty yards from the western rampart, they set their gear down behind a tree. From here they could also keep watch on the bateau.

For a long time the trio kept their eyes fixed on the fort, alert for any moving figure or signs of activity. Their ears strained for any suspicious sound, such as the clank of shovels or picks.

Only the noise of summer insects broke the silence. Chet shifted to a more comfortable position.

"Don't even hear a drumbeat," he said in a re-assured tone.

The Hardys were beginning to feel discouraged when Chet whispered, "What's that?" He inched closer to his pals. "L-listen!"

The boughs above them thrashed in a gust of wind. But the Hardys could also hear a hollow, echoing, breathlike sound from the fort!

"Maybe only wind—along the moat," Frank reasoned, listening as the wind died down. The strange sound subsided, but was still audible.

"Wind! I've never heard wind like that!" Joe whispered. "Unless it's coming through the holes and notches in the walls. It sounds like a seashell when you hold it up to your ear."

"I know what it is—a ghost breathing!" Chet muttered.

The vigil continued until the boys' eyes ached. Finally the three campers decided to sleep in turns. Past midnight, the wind became stronger and the moon broke through the clouds.

As it did, Frank stiffened at something strange on the fort wall. It looked like a skull!

But it proved to be only an area of gutted masonry with spaces resembling eye sockets and teeth.

Later, Chet took his turn on watch and propped himself against the tree. "So far nothing suspicious," he thought, relaxing. One second later he suddenly froze.

Thump! Thump! Drumbeats!

His breath locked tight, Chet sat up, trying to detect the direction of the sound.

Thump! Silence. *Thump!*

Frantically he shook Frank and Joe awake. "What is it?" they asked, immediately alert.

Above the sighing wind, the Hardys clearly heard the drumbeats. They were not coming from the fort but from somewhere near the lake!

Leaping to their feet, they looked down the moonlit water. Frank scanned the calm expanse.

"Look—out there!"

A hooded black figure was gliding towards shore!

Joe, unable to believe what he saw, was the first to gasp:

"*It's a g-ghost—walking on the water!*"

· 16 ·

The Deserted Cottage

THE black, billowing figure glided over the moonlit lake, its wind-blown shroud trailing a shimmering shadow.

For moments Frank, Joe, and Chet remained transfixed until Joe cried, "Come on!"

The Hardys raced down the slope. Chet, although shaking with fear, stumbled after them.

The ghost, its draped arms outstretched, was already nearing shore. The boys saw it disappear beneath overhanging trees beyond the fort promontory.

They ran back for torches, then hurried downhill to the area where the spectre had vanished. But it was nowhere to be seen.

"I still don't believe it!" Frank said. "Maybe I was just having a nightmare."

"Not unless we all had the same one," Joe said. "We all saw that—*thing*."

"But—walking on water!" Chet exclaimed, shivering. "Nobody'll believe us."

"Listen—the drumbeats have stopped!" Frank said. They checked the bateau, found nothing disturbed, and returned to their post on the slope.

Hoping to get another glimpse of the ghost, all three remained awake for some time. But the phantom did not reappear. Near dawn the boys finally fell asleep.

They awoke several hours later, took a dip in the lake, and had breakfast. A search along the shore turned up no clues. Eager to report their experience, they returned to Millwood. Mr Davenport and Uncle Jim were incredulous when they related their ghost story.

The art patron looked hard at the boys. "You all aren't pulling an old Confederate's leg, are you?"

"Oh, no! We saw it. Honest!" Chet said earnestly.

"Sir," said Joe, "this ghost walker wasn't another—er—lake monster, was it?"

"No. At least, not mine."

"We'll keep at our investigation," Frank assured him.

Later in the morning they told Uncle Jim about seeing Ronnie Rush near the fort. The instructor said that Ronnie had not appeared for any of his classes the day before. "Maybe he's still sore about losing out at the exhibition," said Joe. "But I wouldn't be surprised if he's after the fort treasure himself."

The boys then showed Uncle Jim the sculpture tool. "It may be Follette's," he said. "I'd like to go with you to see him, but I'm getting ready for a class."

He filled two bowls from a glass turpentine container, then placed several brushes in one. He was about to dip his paint-covered hands into the other when Joe dashed over and grabbed his wrists.

"Don't!"

"What's the matter?"

Joe pointed to the bowl containing the brushes. "Look!"

Faint smoke rose from it. They all could see the brushes disintegrating!

"That's not turpentine—it's an acid!" Frank cried out.

Mr Kenyon sniffed the liquid. "You're right! Somebody must have put it in the turpentine bottle during the night!"

"Could it have been just a mistake?" Chet asked.

"I'm afraid not. I've never had any reason to keep acid here." He thanked Joe for his quick action, then asked the Hardys, "Do you think whoever did this caused the other accidents and left the shotgun warning?"

"Yes," Frank said. "Or else a confederate. But I doubt that any of the students are involved except maybe Ronnie Rush."

Joe looked thoughtful. "One thing is sure. It's someone who knows his way around here—night or day." The Hardys and Chet left, and went to the sculpture studio. They drew René Follette aside and showed him the initialled tool.

"Yes, yes, it is mine!" he said readily. "It has been missing—oh, maybe two days. Where did you find it?"

The sculptor gave a start when the boys mentioned the mysterious flags at Senandaga but denied any knowledge of them.

Feeling it wise not to reveal details of their visits to Senandaga, the boys left. Outside, Frank said, "Follette didn't act guilty. Perhaps someone stole his knife."

The Hardys debated their next move, eventually deciding to do some detecting on the property of both Gilman and the English hermit.

"I still think there's something fishy about Everett's wet boat."

"And Gilman," Joe added. "He might have had his own reasons for getting hold of the Davenport paintings!"

They divided forces. Joe and Chet would go in the bateau to scout Turtle Island. Frank got permission to borrow the limousine to visit Gilman's estate.

"Here are the keys, sir," said Alex, outside the mansion garage.

Frank thanked him and soon was driving north. He parked in a wooded spot, and trudged along the overgrown shore. Soon he reached the Gilman property.

The Tudor house, as well as the lake-front patio, looked deserted. Circling the grounds convinced Frank that Gilman was not at home.

His ears keen for the sound of a car on the driveway, Frank peered into the ground floor windows. If Gilman were behind the gallery thefts, where might he hide the paintings?

"The attic or the cellar!" Frank thought, wishing it were possible to search these places.

He found the garage open and looked around inside. Nothing suspicious there. Next, Frank pressed his face against a cellar window but saw only garden furniture, tools, and piles of old newspapers. Feeling thwarted, Frank then walked to the lake front. Through a grove of willows to the right, he noticed a boathouse and a long dock.

"I'll check there," he decided, and followed a path through the woods. Suddenly Frank heard footsteps behind him. He was about to spin round when he was struck hard on the head.

Frank's legs turned to rubber and everything went black.

When he came to with a throbbing headache, he he no idea how much time had elapsed since he had passed out. Sensations spun through his consciousness . . . a strong, acrid smell . . . hushed voices . . . echoing . . . a feeling of being adrift.

Suddenly he felt a trickle of water on his face. Frank opened his eyes to darkness. He was encased in something made of metal.

Then he saw jagged holes of light above his head. A chill of horror jolted him!

He was trapped in a steel barrel!

Frantically, Frank tried to turn over. But the container rolled with his movement, forcing water in through the holes.

The steel drum was sinking in the lake!

· 17 ·

The Accused

FRANK kicked at the bottom of the container, then gagged as water rose over his chin.

Spluttering, he pounded his heels against the steel, but it was no use!

In a last desperate effort Frank gave a mighty push upward with his head and hands. The top gave a little. He pushed again, this time loosening the lid enough to free himself. His lungs at the bursting point, Frank swam away from the sinking trap and shot to the surface.

Gasping and gulping in air, he found himself about fifty yards offshore from the limousine.

No boats were in sight as he made it to the shore and collapsed, exhausted. As soon as his strength returned, he stood up and looked about for signs of his attackers. "Maybe someone is hiding in the boat-house," he thought. Frank headed for the building, moving with caution. Finding the padlock open, he slipped inside.

Gilman's lavish craft swayed gently in its berth. Frank peered about the dim interior but saw no one lurking in the shadows. He kicked at a tarpaulin, uncovering a pile of wood moulding. "Wonder what they're for," he mused, and picked up several pieces.

Underneath lay a familiar-looking, ridged strip. It had a diamond-shaped corner!

"It's part of an old fort frame!" Other fragments also appeared to be from the Prisoner-Painter's originals. "Gilman!"

The evidence pointed to the critic as the thief. But Frank was puzzled. Would Gilman have gone so far as to try to drown him?

"The police should know about this immediately," he decided, covering the frames. He ran to the limousine and drove directly to the school. He called the chief, who sent officers Bilton and Turner to meet him at Gilman's. After changing clothes, Frank went back to the critic's house. To his surprise, Gilman was there.

"What is the meaning of this?" the owner demanded as Frank and the policemen approached.

"We'd like to take a look inside your boathouse," said Officer Turner. He showed a search warrant.

Gilman climbed to his feet, his face a mixture of alarm and bewilderment. "Why? What—?"

"Because this young man tells us some stolen property is in there."

"Which I discovered," Frank added, "after someone knocked me out and tried to sink me in a steel drum."

Gilman was flabbergasted. "I'm not guilty of such a terrible thing," he protested. "I'll have you know I am a reputable citizen."

"Come along with us," Officer Turner ordered.

Inside the boathouse, Frank pointed out the diamond-shaped piece of wood. "Recognize that, Mr Gilman?"

"Of course. It looks like an original frame for a Davenport painting."

"Yes. A stolen frame," Frank challenged. "Maybe

you can tell us what it's doing in your boathouse?"

The critic threw up his hands. "I don't know how any of this wood got in here. I am innocent of these hideous accusations. My driver, who also pilots the cruiser, can testify to that. He's been with me for the last few hours."

The driver was questioned closely. He provided a perfect alibi and vehemently denied any part in the attack on Frank. He also maintained that the stack of wood had not been in the boathouse earlier that day.

After searching the premises for the stolen paintings, the officers decided to recover the drum. Frank offered to dive for it, so the three took the rowing-boat to the spot where he had surfaced. Stripping to his shorts, Frank plunged overboard and streaked downwards. Fortunately the water was clear, and he soon spotted the drum, and the lid near it, resting on the sandy bottom at a depth of ten feet.

When Frank bobbed up bearing the evidence, he was helped aboard and the trio returned to the boathouse. The critic paled when he saw his address printed on the side of the drum. "That contained insecticide," he said. "We used up the last of it a week ago."

Gilman looked completely deflated and his chin slumped to his chest. "I didn't have anything to do with this fiendish thing," he muttered.

The officers ordered him not to leave the premises. "You'll have to stay here until we find out the truth," said Turner. He and Bilton took the container and pieces of frame as evidence. By now, Frank had dried off in the hot sun and dressed, so they drove back in the limousine.

"You're lucky to be alive," Bilton remarked.

Frank nodded. "I'm thankful that lid wasn't put on any tighter," he replied. He remembered the voices he had heard just before sinking. "There must have been two men at least."

"At any rate, this is pretty heavy evidence against Gilman," said Turner.

Chet, Joe, Uncle Jim, and Mr Davenport were first stunned, then angered upon hearing of Frank's experience. He had told them his story in the art patron's study. The elderly Southerner kept muttering, "I know Chauncey Gilman's dead set against me—but this—this is incredible."

"I feel the same way," Frank said. "I don't believe he's to blame."

Joe agreed. "If Mr Gilman was so shook up by a fake monster," he said wryly, "I can't see him having the nerve to do anything criminal."

"How about the paintings?" Jim Kenyon asked.

"Not a sign," Frank replied.

"Do you think Gilman knows anything about that ghost we saw last night?" Chet put in.

Frank shrugged. "Remember, Adrian Copler's still at large, and his partners. If we only had some leads to their identity!"

Joe reported that he and Chet had found Turtle Island deserted. Everett and his boat were gone. There was no trace of the stolen paintings.

"His dog was there, but chained up, lucky for us," Chet added.

Mr Davenport declared he himself would visit Chauncey Gilman that afternoon. "I don't like him, but I won't judge him guilty till it's proved."

The boys had a late lunch, after which Frank suggested revisiting the fort. "We can give the interior a good going-over this time," he said.

Jim Kenyon offered to accompany the boys, since he had the afternoon free.

"Swell," said Joe. "We could use a hand combing the fort."

After getting some digging tools, they climbed into the bateau and set off. When they reached Senandaga, the foursome went directly through the entrance tunnel. Pausing in the middle of the parade ground, Frank took out their map.

"Let's see. We're facing south." He pointed to a long, roofless building to his right. "That must be the West Barracks—"

"Or what's left of it," Chet interrupted.

"—And the ruin behind us—here—the North Barracks. This building to our left was for officers. Other than the two demilunes outside, the four corner bastions, and the ramparts themselves, that's the set-up above ground."

"How about the dungeons?" Joe asked. "Jason Davenport must have been kept prisoner in one."

Frank turned the map round. "They were under the West Barracks." They walked over to the stone structure, which rose just above the rampart. Rubble clogged an entrance which evidently led underground.

"It'll be a job getting down there," Frank said.

"Of course, General Davenport likely had the run of the fort," Mr Kenyon reminded them. "He could have found the *chaîne d'or* anywhere."

They decided to comb the barrack ruins first, Frank

taking the one to the west, Joe the old officers' building, and Chet and Uncle Jim the North Barracks.

Originally three-storied, these were now little more than shells with empty window and door frames. Two bleak chimneys remained standing.

Joe climbed through a broken wall section and began searching among the chunks of stone and mortar, most of it from the fallen upper floor.

Hours passed as the boys and Jim worked. Senandaga echoed with the sound of shovels and shifting stones. Each began to doubt the clue could ever be found. What if it were hopelessly buried?

"Look, here's an old sword blade!" Frank called out.

"Great!" Chet responded. "We've just found a rusted grapeshot rack!"

Joe later uncovered a wooden canteen almost intact. But none of them saw anything resembling a tomahawk or a chain. Finally the weary searchers took a break, relaxing on the shore near the bateau.

Suddenly they were startled by men's angry shouts from inside the fort!

Frank and Joe, followed by Chet and his uncle, ran up the slope and through the tunnel, then halted in amazement.

At one side of the parade ground, two men were furiously exchanging blows!

· 18 ·

A Sudden Disappearance

"René Follette and Lloyd Everett!" cried Frank in astonishment.

The Hardys, Chet, and Jim Kenyon rushed over and separated the fighting men. Mr Kenyon silenced them. "What's this all about, René?"

"This hermit—he insults my ancestor, the great Marquis de Chambord!"

Everett snorted. "Who was brought to heel by *my* forebear, Lord Craig!"

"Then it's *you* two who have been raising the French and British flags," Frank declared.

Reluctantly, first Everett, then Follette admitted having done so to have his country's flag flying for Senandaga Day. Each man had lowered the other's banner, but neither had been looking for the golden chain. Each had, however, come at various times to search for proof of his ancestor's victory.

René grunted. "You, Everett, struck me unconscious last Tuesday!"

"Utter nonsense! Besides—you struck *me* cold yesterday!"

"A lie!"

The Hardys exchanged glances. Who had knocked out the Englishman and the sculptor? Frank asked them if they had seen a black-robed "ghost" around the fort.

"Ghost, no!" Follette waved emphatically. "But I still feel that blow on my head!"

Jim Kenyon, with some difficulty, got the two to shake hands and declare a truce.

After the men had pushed off in their boats, the boys and Uncle Jim resumed their explorations, skirting the ramparts. Frank and Joe noticed small openings at foot level along the entire parapet, evidently rifle ports to reinforce cannon fire. But looking through one, Joe found it obstructed.

"Look!" he called to his brother. "Somebody's wedged a tin can in here! And in the next opening, too!"

Frank found the same thing true along the north rampart.

"This explains the eerie noise of the wind we heard!" he said. "These might have been stuck in to make the spooky sounds!"

Suddenly he knelt down and yanked out a rectangular can from one port. Joe sniffed at the open top. "This held paraffin!" he exclaimed. He pulled the cork from his pocket. It fitted perfectly.

Frank held on to the tin. Crouching, the Hardys moved along the notched wall guarding the fort. Bend by bend, they checked for markings or loose stones.

"Let's try the demilunes," Frank urged at last.

They were just crossing the wooden planking to the southern demilune when Chet's voice rang out.

"Frank—Joe—Uncle Jim, come here!"

Rushing down to the end of the North Barracks,

the others found Chet holding up a piece of black cloth. Excitedly the Hardys examined it.

"Frank—you think—?"

"It's from the ghost? Could be!"

Jim Kenyon took the torn fragment and rubbed his fingers over the cloth.

He looked at the boys. "If so, your ghost got his costume from Millwood! This is a piece of a painting smock—dyed!"

He pointed out white markings still faintly visible beneath the black dye. They spelled "Mil."

"Wow!" Chet burst out. "You think the phantom is an artist?"

"Whatever he is," Joe said, "how did he walk on water?"

Frank showed Chet and his uncle the paraffin tin, and told of the other cans he and Joe had found. "They look like fruit-juice cans," he added. "Maybe someone bought supplies in Cedartown."

"Like Adrian Copler!" Joe ventured. "Or a crony. I'll bet that thief is in hiding near Senandaga."

Although disappointed at not unearthing the treasure clue, they felt encouraged by Chet's discovery, and the Hardys resolved to try tracking down the owner of the piece of smock.

They had just pulled up the bateau on the Millwood beach when Alex the chauffeur came running towards them, a troubled expression on his face.

"What's the matter?" asked Uncle Jim.

"Have any of you seen Mr Davenport?"

They shook their heads. "No, we just came from the fort," Frank answered. "Why?"

"He had me drive him to Mr Gilman's early this

afternoon," Alex reported, worriedly fingering his cap. "Mr Davenport was to phone me to pick him up before dinner-time. It's past that now, and I haven't heard a word!"

"Do you think something has happened to him?" Joe asked.

"I just telephoned Mr Gilman. He told me he hasn't seen Mr Davenport." Alex added that the art patron had got out of the car on the road just before the critic's property.

"Could Gilman be lying?" Chet put in.

"Let's find out," Joe urged.

Hastily leaving their gear outside the mansion, the boys jumped into the limousine and drove to Gilman's home. The man appeared completely bewildered. "I don't know what's going on," he whined. "Everything is blamed on me."

A thorough search of the grounds proved futile. There was no sign of Jefferson Davenport. Next the Hardys and Chet made inquiries in town. No one there had seen the man, nor could any of the Millwood students provide the boys with a clue.

By midnight, with still no word of the millionaire, Chet's uncle telephoned police headquarters. The chief said a missing-person alarm would be sent out.

Next morning the school buzzed with the news of Mr Davenport's disappearance. The Hardys felt that there was a strong link between it and the art thefts.

"It could be a desperate move by Copler and his gang to get information about the treasure," Frank said. "I move we check the fort again. If that's their hideout, they may be questioning Mr Davenport there."

The hatchet narrowly missed Frank's head!

Joe and Chet agreed, and the three hurriedly took off in the bateau.

Once inside Senandaga, they searched for the millionaire. Finding no sign of him above ground, they decided to tackle the dungeon entrances. There were two in the West and two in the North Barracks. "Let's try the north first," said Frank. The opening was blocked by what seemed tons of rubble. The old steps were barely visible.

"How'll we ever dig through this stuff!" Chet groaned.

The boys found many of the rocks too large to be moved with shovels. In minutes their faces were covered with perspiration.

They tried the second north entrance. Here they found decayed timber poking out of the rocks. Frank and Chet lifted out a rotting door and set it against a wall.

The diggers proceeded, making a little headway.

Suddenly they heard a splintering thud. The boys whirled to see a hatchet embedded in the old door! It had narrowly missed Frank's head!

"Who threw that?" Joe yelled angrily.

"Look!" Chet quavered, pointing.

They saw, fleeing out the main gateway, a hooded black figure!

The three boys raced in pursuit.

"You two go that way!" Frank yelled, jumping into the ditch and running off to the left. Chet and Joe sped in the opposite direction.

But they circled the fort walls without spotting the ghostly figure. Back at the digging site, Joe pulled the hatchet from the door. "It's an ordinary camping type, but I'm glad we weren't in its way!"

Frank studied the broad blade of the axe, then took out the photostat of the fort map and spread it on the ground.

"What's up?" Joe asked curiously.

"Look at this hatchet," Frank urged, "then at the shape of any side of the fort!"

Joe looked at the eastern rampart on the map as his brother's hand covered one of the corner bastions. "It's like a tomahawk!" he exclaimed. "It must be the clue painted by General Davenport!"

The three boys were greatly excited. "Which side of the fort is the right one, though?" Chet puzzled.

"In the painting the tomahawk was parallel to the west wall! And remember the notches on it near the end of the stock?" said Frank.

"The West Barracks!" Joe said. "The notches must refer to one of the dungeon cells! But that hatchet-throwing ghost—could *he* know about this clue?"

"I doubt it," Frank said. "He was trying to scare us out of this fort, but the joke may be on him. If we're right, he gave us a swell lead. Maybe we can find Mr Davenport and the treasure too! Come on!"

Grabbing their shovels, the three moved over to the West Barracks, at the entrance nearest the notches shown in the picture. Spurred by renewed hope, they worked furiously.

An hour later Frank managed to wriggle through a hole they had opened in the rubble. Joe and Chet watched tensely as he lowered himself into blackness.

"It's all right!" Frank called.

The others passed the shovels down and joined Frank. Chet squeezed through with the Hardys' help. The boys switched on their torches and found themselves in a long, dark corridor, partially filled with debris.

A row of cells extended along the left wall. The Hardys were eager to explore and started for the nearest cell. Together, the boys inspected one dungeon after another, their rotting wood doors sagging on rusty iron hinges.

Frank and Chet were playing their lights on the floor of the fourth cell when Joe shouted from behind them, "Look—on the back wall!"

His beam focused on faint scratch marks in the stone.

The boys hurried over. Now they saw the scratches formed a definite shape: a broad blade, notched handle, and an encircling chain—identical to the one in the Davenport painting!

"This must have been the Prisoner-Painter's cell!" Frank exclaimed.

They felt the wall with their fingers. Joe frowned. "Solid as steel," he commented. "How about the floor?"

Frank kicked aside the remains of what had been the prisoner's bed. As his foot touched one of the floor stones, it rattled!

"Joe—a shovel!"

Prodding with the spade, Frank levered the large slab, and the others lifted it out. Their torches revealed a gaping hole!

· 19 ·

Dungeon Trap

"It's not very deep." Frank crouched. "I'll go first."

The Hardys dropped down into the opening and beamed their lights around.

"It's a tunnel!" Joe hissed.

Behind them was a stone wall, but ahead stretched a low, earth passageway. Chet lowered shovels and all three moved forward, ducking their heads.

"Easy—this ceiling doesn't look safe," Frank cautioned. "I don't get it. We're going west, which means the chain must be hidden outside the fort. Why?"

"Beats me," Joe replied.

There appeared to be no turns. Farther on, they were surprised to find the tunnel angling downhill, then realized this was because of the fort ditch above.

Suddenly the trio were brought up short by a wall of dirt. Joe whispered, "Do you think it's the end, or a cave-in?"

Frank probed the sloping earth with his spade. "It looks like a cave-in, and a big one."

The three debated about digging through the dirt barrier.

"We'll be risking another cave-in," Frank said. "If only we knew whether or not this tunnel continues. And if it does, where to."

"Let's chance it," Joe urged.

The Bayport sleuths set their torches on the floor and began shovelling with utmost care.

Beneath its hard-packed outer layer, the dirt was loose. The boys dumped spadeful after spadeful to one side. Suddenly they stopped digging, and listened, motionless.

Stealthy footsteps were approaching!

Grabbing a torch, Joe swung the beam back down the passage. It fell on the face of a tall, sullen-faced youth.

"Ronnie Rush!"

"Well, I finally caught up to you three. I hitched a ride in a motorboat, and trailed you here to the fort. Did you find the gold chain?"

Ronnie, striding forward defiantly, forgot to duck. His head struck the low ceiling. A thunderous sound followed as the tunnel walls gave way.

"Look out!" Frank cried.

Ronnie leaped ahead. He and the boys went down beneath a barrage of falling earth. Choking dust filled the tunnel. Joe staggered to his feet and thrust a shovel into the mass of earth. "Frank! We're cut off!"

The Hardys dug furiously, but it was no use. They were sealed in!

"There's not enough air to last the four of us even a couple of hours!" Frank warned. "So every move will have to count."

Chet glowered at Rush, who lay stunned. "If it weren't for you—"

"You really scored this time, Rush," Frank agreed. "But we can't waste air arguing about it."

"I'm—I'm sorry," Ronnie said, contrite for the first time. "I was wrong to snoop, and steal your fort map. I had overheard Mr Davenport and Mr Kenyon talking about this treasure, and that you fellows were coming up here and—"

"You knocked me out to get our map," Joe finished.

Ronnie shook his head, puzzled. "No! I took the map, but I don't know anything about knocking you out—honest!"

As the youth seemed genuinely contrite, the other boys exchanged glances. If he hadn't struck Joe, who had? Ronnie looked fearfully round at the enclosing walls.

"I just want to say, in case we—we don't get out of here, I—uh—well, I'm really sorry about Chet's painting and all—"

"Right now, you can be our shovel relief," Frank said tersely.

First the boys recovered their torches, then they dug steadily. When Chet collapsed with fatigue, Rush took up his shovel. The three lights cut bright spears through the small black space. Breathing was difficult and their clothes were drenched from exertion.

"Come on! We've got to get through!" Ronnie panted.

Seconds later, Joe's shovel pierced the barrier and a cool draught hit their hot faces.

"We've made it!" Frank shouted.

The boys clawed rapidly with their tools, cutting a wider opening. Then they ducked through in single file and advanced slowly; their torches beamed ahead. A short distance farther on was a wall with openings to the right and left.

"I'll bet these are infiltration tunnels!" Joe exclaimed.

They entered the opening to the right, and found it littered with old French weapons, including rusty muskets and three small cannon, but as Frank feared, the tunnel ended in a solid blank wall.

The searchers hastily returned to enter the left-hand opening.

"Frank, how far out from the fort wall do you think we are?" Chet asked.

"Maybe a hundred yards west, probably to the woods. What an ingenious idea—if Chambord ever did use this for infiltration!"

He recalled Mr Davenport's mention of the Vauban parallel trenches, once used by attacking armies to close in on fortresses. Had Chambord reversed this idea, building these tunnels for defence?

Fifty yards farther ahead, they reached another dirt wall.

"There's got to be a way out!" Frank reasoned. "Let's try the wall."

They spread out, and with Chet holding the lights, gently probed the dry earth. Minutes later, a section fell away under Ronnie's shovel.

"Here it is!"

Carefully widening the hole just enough, they ducked quickly through and proceeded down a tunnel heading back towards the fort.

"It's parallel to the other," Joe observed.

Presently they came to the beginning of the passageway—a wall of dirt.

"Funny," said Frank. "The other tunnel started from a stone wall."

Just then Joe flashed his light above and exclaimed, "Look!"

The beam revealed a square slab of stone. Hopefully the boys pushed it up and minutes later climbed out to find themselves in another cell. Covered with grime, the companions trudged along the dungeon corridor, and picked their way through the debris outside the entrance. They emerged on the parade ground again as dusk was falling.

Suddenly Frank spotted a uniformed man standing at the fort entrance. He ran towards them.

"Alex!" Frank cried out.

"Thank goodness you're safe!" the chauffeur exclaimed. "Mr Davenport has been found. He's with Mr Kenyon right now!"

"Where?" Frank asked.

"Come with me!" Alex led them across to the North Barracks, where an opening had now been cleared through a dungeon entrance—the same where the boys had started digging before the hatchet was thrown. "Mr Kenyon found him down here—he's not well!"

Concerned, they slid below, where several lanterns illuminated a dank corridor. The boys stared in amazement at two figures at the far end. One was Jefferson Davenport, propped against the wall with his legs bound. The other was a short, pug-faced man who held a rock over Mr Davenport's head.

"Adrian Copler!" Joe exclaimed. "Why, you—" Stepping forward, he was blocked by Alex!

"One move, my young Mr Hardy," he said, smiling coldly, "and Davenport is done for."

As Copler swung the rock menacingly, the chauffeur

thrust Frank back. "All of you—on your stomachs on the floor!"

"Why—you're in with them!" Chet muttered incredulously.

"Shut up!" Alex barked.

The boys exchanged hopeless glances, and in order to spare Mr Davenport, submitted to being tied hand and foot. Then Alex dragged his four prisoners roughly along and pushed them against the wall a short distance from the millionaire.

"I told you we'd get 'em!" Alex said. "Those snooping Hardys!"

"Good work!"

A hooded black figure appeared out of the shadows. Spellbound, the boys heard a soft laugh, then saw a gloved hand whisk down the hood to reveal a bearded, hawk-nosed face.

Myles Warren!

· 20 ·

The Final Link

THE trapped boys stared at Warren in astonishment, hardly able to believe their eyes.

"Then you, Alex, and Copler have been behind the painting thefts *and* the haunted fort!" Joe exclaimed.

"No doubt you're surprised," Warren answered with an irritating air of superiority. "Too bad you had to find out. But you may be able to tell us more than stupid Copler."

The art thief flushed. "Oh, yeah? You haven't been holed up in this miserable dungeon—all because of that worthless junk!"

He jerked a thumb over his shoulder. It was then, in the dimness, that the boys noticed a stack of paintings, some without frames, against the wall farther up the corridor. The stolen fort pictures!

"Shut up!" Warren snapped at his partner. "You talk too much!"

"Alex, it was you who kidnapped Mr Davenport for the treasure clue," Frank prodded. "Where does Gilman fit in?"

Warren laughed. "He doesn't. After we failed to find any clues in the old frames, we removed several in order to 'frame' Gilman, so to speak." The merchant went on to admit being the ringleader, and that he and Alex had put Frank in the steel drum.

"We didn't intend to drown you," Alex put in. "That's why we didn't put the lid on tight."

The sports-shop owner had quickly engineered the fake detour after Alex informed him that the boys were heading for the fort that night. Warren also had been responsible for the canoe sabotage, as well as the dock fire. It was Alex who had learned the Hardys had been asked to come to Millwood.

"No doubt you, Alex, and Warren stole all the fort paintings from the gallery," Frank said.

Warren nodded, boasting, "Pretty clever I was to get into Millwood by playing the weekend painter bit."

He said that the red paint smear had accidentally been rubbed off from his artist's smock on to the back of the picture while he had been examining it in the gallery.

"And of course you had a good chance to shotgun that red paint into our room," Joe said.

"Naturally." Warren's eyes glittered. "I trust you remember that message I left."

The Hardys and Chet felt a chill of fear as they recalled the ominous threat.

Ronnie spoke up. "Joe, he must be the one who hit you on the head!"

Warren glared. "And you must be the twerp who beat us to that map!"

"Did you push my car down the slope?" Chet asked. Warren pointed to the chauffeur.

"My orders, of course, though your pal was lucky enough to foul them up. Alex tells me he gave you three quite a runaround in the woods one night."

Not to be outdone, Alex boasted of cutting the ferry cables. "We had to do something to discourage tourist pests. Unfortunately that zany Frenchman and Everett kept nosing around the fort—they had lumps on their heads to show for it."

"By the way," Copler whined proudly, "those well boards didn't move by themselves. You Hardy pests kept me cooped up that day, but I sneaked out once."

The boys learned that the drumbeats were made by Copler who had used an Indian tomtom to signal his partners for meetings.

"What have you done to Mr Davenport?" Frank demanded, worried because of the elderly man's silence and drawn face.

"He hasn't been co-operative." Warren smirked. "He'll get worse treatment if you don't tell us where the gold chain is hidden!"

Even Chet now realized they must play for time. "One thing that still puzzles me," he said, "is how you walked on the lake on Monday night. It was great."

"Simple," Warren bragged, holding up two black slotted objects resembling small surfboards. "Water shoes, made of urethane. Copler trimmed 'em down. By the way"—he chuckled—"Alex provided Kenyon with a little acid 'turpentine—' "

"You lost out there, Warren," Joe taunted. "We already uncovered that."

Warren became furious. He struck Joe across the face. "Wise guy! What's that painting clue? When you almost dug into our set-up here, Copler overheard you say something about a tomahawk—what? Better still, where's that gold chain?"

"We don't know yet—we've been looking in a tunnel," Frank said.

"Tunnel? Where?" Alex demanded. "You've got a lead—out with it!"

The Hardys explained the clue, adding that Warren's hatchet had given them the lead. "The west dungeons, either entrance," Joe said. "There are loose cell stones. One tunnel leads to a cave-in. We can show you."

"No you don't!" Warren said harshly, satisfied with the information. He picked up two lanterns.

"Copler, you stay here and keep your eye on these kids. Alex, we're going for that chain!"

After Warren and the chauffeur had left, Frank racked his brain for a way to escape. Joe looked over and shrugged. Adrian Copler boasted, "You fools should have paid attention to my warning in Bayport. You'll be sorry you didn't!"

A few minutes later Copler began pacing the room nervously. Frank glanced at Mr Davenport, who winked and signalled the boy closer.

Though bound hand and foot, Frank inched along the floor until he was two feet from the millionaire. Suddenly Davenport moaned and slumped over. In alarm Copler rushed to him.

"Davenport! What's happened? Don't die! Please. Not here!"

All the while Frank was pulling his knees up until he was poised like a spring.

Wham! His feet flew forward and caught Copler on the side of the head. The thief collapsed like an empty sack.

Instantly the millionaire opened his eyes and smiled.

"Good work!" He untied Frank, who promptly released the others. As they freed Mr Davenport's legs, he assured them he was all right. He chuckled. "Some act I put on, eh?"

Ronnie agreed to stay with him while the Hardys and Chet went after Alex and Warren. The Bayporters emerged and crossed the vacant parade ground to the West Barracks. "They could have gone in either one," Frank surmised. "Let's check the first!"

They squirmed below and crept along the silent corridor into the clue-marked cell. Frank switched off his light before dropping soundlessly into the hole at the beginning of the tunnel. Chet followed, then Joe.

They listened carefully before flashing on their torches. The lights hit the barrier of caved-in dirt sixty feet ahead. Nobody in sight.

"They must be in the other tunnel," Joe said, and turned about. "Come on!" But his attention was suddenly caught by a straight fissure in the stone wall at the start of the tunnel. On a sudden hunch Joe grasped a projecting stone edge and he tugged with both hands. Frank did the same. The stone moved slightly. Excited, the Hardys pulled with all their might. Finally a door creaked open!

"What do you know about that!" Chet exclaimed.

Cautiously they stepped inside a paved passageway.

Wondering if they would meet Warren and Alex, the three boys followed the newly found tunnel beneath the fort interior. At its end, they played their torches round a large chamber.

Frank spotted a glitter of metal and followed it with the ray from his torch. Link by link, a huge gold chain was revealed, hanging majestically round the vault!

"The treasure!" Joe exclaimed. "We've found it!"

"And look at this," said Frank, pointing to a dusty book and tomahawk on a table.

"I knew the Prisoner-Painter had a reason for putting the clue in that one cell!" Joe said.

The boys were curious about the book, but Frank rushed the others back into the passage. "Let's get to that other tunnel!"

They went up to the second dungeon entrance and slipped down to the cell above the tunnel. The stone had been pushed aside from the hole.

"Quiet!" Frank whispered, turning off his light. They dropped below and tensely moved forward into the darkness. After a while they saw a lantern flash ahead!

"Get down!" Joe whispered. They dropped to their stomachs, hearing first Alex's voice, then Warren's.

"But the kid said something about a cave-in down there to the right—it's a dead end."

"You're crazy—the cave-in's the other way!" Warren retorted. "There must be a link-up in this direction."

"I say left," the chauffeur persisted.

As the men's voices rose in argument, Chet and the Hardys crept closer.

"Suit yourself," Warren said finally, "I'm trying the right. Yell if you find it." Their footsteps receded. Frank signalled the others to their feet.

"They've separated—let's take Warren first!"

With Joe remaining on guard, Frank and Chet turned down to the right, moving along opposite walls.

When they reached the pale glow of Warren's lantern, Frank jumped him.

Startled, Warren wrenched him off and swung his lantern. He was about to bring it down on Frank's head when Chet tackled him.

"Alex!"

Warren's cry echoed as he kicked Chet away, only to reel staggering into the wall from Frank's smashing uppercut. A second punch dropped him unconscious before Alex rushed out of the shadows.

"Why, you—" As the man lurched towards Frank, Joe caught him from behind with a stinging bang on the left ear. Enraged and thrown off balance, Alex threw a backhand blow. Joe ducked it and at the same time Frank swung a roundhouse right. It landed on the point of Alex's jutting chin. Out cold, he fell face forward on the tunnel floor.

As Frank rubbed his bruised knuckles, Chet and Joe bound the captives with belts.

"Wow! You really bombed him," Chet praised Frank. "Hey, what's that noise?"

They left the conspirators and hurried outside to the parade ground. Mr Kenyon rushed up to them, followed by half a dozen policemen!

"Frank! Chet! Joe! You're a sight for sore eyes! Did you find Mr Davenport?"

"Yes. He's okay." Chet grinned. "We have three prisoners, too."

Rapidly the boys related their amazing adventure, ending with outwitting the thieves.

"I knew something was fishy when you didn't get back to Millwood," Uncle Jim explained, "especially after the housekeeper said Alex had gone to look for Mr Davenport, and never showed up again."

He expressed astonishment at Warren and Alex being in cahoots with Copler, and surmised that the chauffeur had forged his references. "But it sounds like Ronnie Rush has reformed a little," he added, smiling.

The Cedartown police chief congratulated the boys, then sent his men below for the prisoners. The Hardys, Chet, and Uncle Jim rejoined Mr Davenport and Ronnie. Grinning, Joe asked the art patron if he could stand another shock.

The elderly Southerner straightened his shoulders. "Reckon so if I can deal with criminals."

With Ronnie meekly trailing behind, the Hardys led the way to the secret chamber beneath the centre of the fort. There the group gazed in awe at the magnificence of the gleaming chain of gold.

"It's beyond words!" Mr Davenport said happily. "Thanks to you detectives, and Jason's clue, this priceless treasure is safe! I'll see that it's properly displayed near the paintings of my esteemed ancestor."

Chet looked slyly at Ronnie. "If I do a painting of the treasure, will you 'help' me win another prize?"

Ronnie grinned sheepishly. "Never again!"

The Hardys then explained their theory about the infiltration tunnels, and Joe pointed out the old book. Mr Davenport leafed through it. He looked up, astonished.

"What you boys have uncovered will rewrite history!" he declared. "This is a ledger left by Chambord hours before he and his garrison evacuated Senandaga, using these tunnels to escape to another battle area. According to this account, he planned to station Iroquois Indians—*disguised as French soldiers*—on the ramparts."

"To decoy Lord Craig!" Frank guessed.

"Precisely."

"Then the men the British attacked were actually *Indians!*" Joe put in, then frowned. "But Follette said 'Frenchmen' had been seen on the ramparts after the English had left."

The boys recalled Everett'sacccount of the "French" fleeing when they could not manage the cannon.

"The disguised Iroquois must have come back!" Chet exclaimed. "Maybe to loot the fort."

Mr Davenport nodded. He said that Craig, after taking the fort, must have suspected the trick, and left immediately. "Chambord's estimate here of the size of the attacking British force seems too large—Craig himself may have played a trick!"

"So the last true holders of Senandaga were the Iroquois!" Joe exclaimed. He held up the tomahawk. "Wait until René Follette and Mr Everett hear about this!"

Frank and Joe looked at the *chaîne d'or* and wondered when another challenge as baffling as the haunted fort would come their way. Sooner than they expected, they would be called upon to solve the *Mystery of the Whale Tattoo.*

Mr Davenport grinned. "I'm hereby inviting you all to celebrate with a hearty Southern repast. How does that sound to you, Chet?"

The stocky boy beamed. "Super! Right now, I could use some *real* fortification!"

Have you read all the adventures in the Armada Hardy Boys series? There are four thrilling mysteries for Frank and Joe—and Chet Morton of course—packed with action and excitement on every page!

The Mystery of the Aztec Warrior
The Arctic Patrol Mystery
The Haunted Fort
The Mystery of the Whale Tattoo

Watch out for Hardy Boys adventures Nos. 5 and 6, coming in Armada in August 1974

The Mystery of the Disappearing Floor
The Mystery of the Melted Coins

If you have enjoyed this book, you will love the adventures of another young detective—Nancy Drew, the red-haired sleuth who just can't help finding mysteries wherever she goes.

There are six Nancy Drew stories in Armada, each one a gripping tale of excitement and danger.

The Secret of Shadow Ranch

The Mystery of the 99 Steps

The Clue in the Crossword Cipher

The Message in the Hollow Oak

The Spider Sapphire Mystery

The Quest of the Missing Map

and there are two new Nancy Drew stories by Carolyn Keene coming in Armada in May 1974

The Clue in the Old Stagecoach

The Clue of the Broken Locket